THE EYE STONES

A shock awaits Deborah Ritchie when she arrives to stay with her recently married sister. She is told that the couple have both perished tragically in a fire which destroyed their home. Alone in the bleak Norfolk brecklands, Deborah is forced to accept hospitality from the forbidding Sir Randall Gaunt. She gladly leaves Sir Randall and his grim anatomical practices for the warm companionship of young Lord Stannard and his family. But before long, she is inextricably involved in a nightmare of mystery and unimagined evil . . .

HARRIET ESMOND

◆

THE EYE STONES

Complete and Unabridged

LINFORD
Leicester

First published in Great Britain

First Linford Edition
published 2018

Copyright © 1975 by Jean Burke
and John Burke
Copyright © 2017 by Jean Burke

A catalogue record for this book is available
from the British Library.

ISBN 978–1–4448–3795–7

Published by
F. A. Thorpe (Publishing)
Anstey, Leicestershire

Set by Words & Graphics Ltd.
Anstey, Leicestershire
Printed and bound in Great Britain by
T. J. International Ltd., Padstow, Cornwall

This book is printed on acid-free paper

1

After so many hours of travelling, her eyes ached, but she was unable to close them. The sombre landscape mesmerised her. More than that: out of that flat uninviting expanse came some whisper that stirred an inexplicable unease in her mind. Something was waiting for her, something she would not wish to face.

This morning Deborah had set out in good spirits, looking forward to seeing Beatrice again. They would talk, she could relax after the weeks of sadness and problems, and even if Beatrice were as flighty and extravagant and self-centred as ever, it would make a wonderful change of mood. Yet now, as the train drew nearer to the junction and their reunion, she was beginning to feel misgivings — to be scared, even. All that time abroad, coping with difficult deci-sions and in the end with the heaviest imaginable responsibility, she had never felt fear. Worry, yes; but never anything like this creeping sense of something somewhere being terribly wrong.

It was hard to picture the exuberant Beatrice fitting contentedly into this bleakness.

The last hour had been particularly depressing, over dull green levels sliced by long ditches, with little light and shade. So different from the wooded hills around Carlsbad where she and her father had spent so much time. In Scotland and in Bohemia the skylines were jagged with hills or forests. Here, on these plains and fens of eastern England, the horizon was no more than a lightly pencilled rim against the sullen September sky. Wind buffeted the train as it slowed across a winding road following some ancient boundary.

A barouche waited on the road, the horse jerking its head away from the noise and smoke of the engine. Deborah sank back, finally letting her eyes close.

Another fifteen minutes and they would reach the junction. Half an hour after that, she would be met at that remote little station, and Beatrice's brittle chatter would blow away any lingering phantoms.

She opened her eyes again.

The middle-aged couple sitting opposite her had obviously just exchanged a glance of mutual understanding. The black merino and Deborah's black bonnet, with the merest trim of grey lace, spoke for themselves. As Deborah rubbed her eyes, the woman took out a smelling-bottle and leaned forward solicitously.

'You're on your way to some sad family occasion?' There was genuine kindness mixed in with her curiosity.

Deborah took the bottle gratefully. 'No, I've left that behind me. I am on my way to stay a short while with relatives. A quiet holiday.'

The gentleman tugged at his silver-streaked beard. Silently he appeared to be commenting that it was a strange region to choose for a recuperative holiday.

'You have come far?' his wife asked.

'From Edinburgh.'

'A long way to come alone.'

3

A touch of disapproval. Respectable young ladies ought not to attempt long journeys without at least a maid.

'I am used to travelling, and to dealing with whatever circumstances may arise.'

The husband risked a faint smile. He probably shared his wife's views, but was yet attracted by her younger, slightly defiant outlook. Deborah had seen that envious, appreciative glint in the expressions of many older men during her travels.

She let her head sink back against the head-rest and gazed once more out of the window. Memories came unsummoned between her and the landscape of the present: memories that would not soon fade. She was exhausted rather than sad; drained, yet still not quite able to believe that she would no longer hear her father calling out in pain, would not have to tuck the rugs about his knees or wheel him to take the waters or help him laboriously from one place to another, one country to another.

She fought down any shameful feeling of liberation. But undoubtedly a weight

4

had been lifted from her. Those final years with her father had not been easy.

The motion of the coach reminded her of so many other trains. For three years she had trailed from one European spa to another. Invalided out of his regiment after wounds received at Ferozeshah on that pitiless December day in 1845, and ravaged by disease following the engagement, Colonel Ritchie battled with illness as gallantly as he had battled in the field. But the failings of his body had brought him sometimes close to despair.

'Go and make a life for yourself, girl.' Deborah heard echoes of his voice, raging against his own infirmity. 'Get me a nurse and be off with you. We'll have an end to this nonsense ... I should have been killed cleanly, like a man.' It was a recurrent theme. 'Not turned out to rot like this. Think on the times I was close to a decent death, something you could have been proud of, and instead you've got this *foul* burden ... '

He would be close to tears, and hating himself for that weakness. The times when he was most insistent that she should leave him were the times when he most needed her.

Now he was the one who had left.

When he died suddenly in Carlsbad, she had had to make all the arrangements for getting him home. Beatrice had of course not sent any offer of help. Deborah could have predicted the content of the two confused letters Beatrice wrote, first to Carlsbad and then to Edinburgh: one commiserating, saying how dreadful it was that they were so far apart and urging her to come and stay after the funeral; the next confirming a week suggested by Deborah, saying any day, any time would be wonderful. She should and simply telegraph the time of her train so that she could be met at the station.

Colonel Ritchie had been interred with full military honours in Edinburgh. From his executors, Deborah discovered herself to be a well-to-do young woman of independent means. The family solicitor had told her: 'So you'd best be careful with yourself, lassie.' She needed time to learn how to cope with that independence — time, and a complete change of scene.

She had telegraphed Beatrice and set off. And here she was, approaching her destination.

The train slowed. There was a scattering of houses, and then they were running in beside a station platform. As they stopped, the gentleman opposite sprang up and took her small bag from the rack. He opened the carriage door and got down to help Deborah out. 'I trust you are being met?'

'I have another short journey to make — a branch line connection to Ingmere.'

'Ingmere?' He had never heard of it. Nor had Deborah herself, until Beatrice wrote inviting her to stay and giving instructions on the route. The first address she had received after Beatrice's impulsive marriage had been in London; then one in Bath; and lastly this remote one.

Her self-appointed protector signalled a porter and despatched him to take her trunk from the luggage van. When they parted he shook hands formally, bowed his head with equal formality to impress his wife rather than Deborah, and climbed back into the compartment with a wistful backward glance.

A few people waited for the connection. Two women sat patiently on a large wickerwork basket. A young man and woman stood near the edge of the platform, urging the train to arrive and carry them away. Another man paced up and down, a measured six steps in each direction, imperceptibly quickening his pace as the moments ticked by. He wore a dark brown paletot with a wide velvet collar, and black trousers. His head was lowered as he stomped to and fro, his dark neatly trimmed side whiskers blending into the collar and narrowing his already lean features. Apparently a man who could not bear to waste a minute of his time.

The six steps in one direction became ten, so that he passed Deborah. As he did so, he glanced indifferently at her; then slowed, stopped, and turned on his heel.

She thought he was about to speak to her. Instead he subjected her to a piercing scrutiny as if demanding where they could have met before. Deborah turned away, hiding her face within the deep scalloped edges of her bonnet.

The branch line train arrived, its high-chimneyed engine rolling a cloud of smoke back into the faces of the two men on the open footplate. Deborah waved to the porter and hurried him towards a compartment away from the stranger's. To her relief, she was joined by two ladies who emerged at the last minute from the waiting-room.

In the thickening twilight, the train rumbled along the edge of a heath. The fitful sun had dodged through most of the afternoon behind a tumult of burnished cloud. Now as it sank, colour faded from the clouds and from the landscape.

This bracken wilderness was even less welcoming than the levels she had so recently crossed. They had at least been green and well irrigated. Here the tracks ran beside tufts and tracts of scrub that swallowed up whatever light there was. A faint spattering against the window seemed to promise a mild shower of rain, but then she saw particles of sand in the grooves of the woodwork, inside and out.

She brushed her hand across her knee and swept prickly grains to the floor. The train progressed into more desolate surroundings. They were travelling into a desert: deep inland yet as sandy as the seashore, with only a few stunted pines along a shallow distant ridge, and untilled wastes littered with white-edged flints.

Abruptly they were in Ingmere station. A few wooden sheds were followed by a row of cottages, and then the platform. Beyond the station fence was huddled a small grey town, barely more than a village.

As Deborah stepped down, she saw the dark man standing on the platform near the exit, staring back in her direction. There was no sign of Beatrice.

One porter stood some distance away. He looked at Deborah but made no move towards her until she lifted her hand. His expression was grudging. But Deborah had grown accustomed to summoning porters and getting what she wanted. As he carried her trunk through the station building, she asked: 'There is a carriage waiting outside?'

'Not that I saw when I came through, miss.'

As she came out on to the forecourt, wind-blown flecks of grit stung her cheek. At first she thought it was more of that sand that had been blown against the train. Then she noticed grey specks on her dark sleeve, and a thicker whitish-grey deposit on the station fence. The harsh dust was blowing from a flintknappers' yard at the foot of the station approach.

The porter set her trunk down and waited for his tip. 'You expecting someone from out of the breck, miss?'

'The breck?'

He waved vaguely over the huddled rooftops. 'Out there. The breckland. Lucky if anyone gets through tonight. Piling up out there, that be. The stage is biding its time. Not likely to risk it.'

She dropped a coin in his palm, and he hurried off to make what he could from another passenger. The dark man passed him in the doorway, carrying only a small valise, and glanced about him impatiently. Clearly he also expected to be met. Rather than become involved with him,

11

Deborah moved a few paces over the cobbles and turned her face away from the cutting wind.

When the porter showed himself again, she called him over. 'My name is Deborah Ritchie. As there is no one to meet me, you are sure there is no message?'

'Nothing here, miss. You'd best ask at the inn.'

Light shone from a window at the foot of the shallow slope, and from a door that opened and shut, opened and shut again.

'Perhaps you'll be good enough to take my trunk inside and look after it until I'm ready.'

Giving him no time to protest, and carrying her reticule and small bag, she went down the slope to the inn beside the knappers' yard. Through the archway into the stable yard she could discern the outline of a stagecoach. An ostler was closing a stable door. Deborah hesitated, then hurried into the yard as the dark man stamped past her and in through the front entrance of the inn.

'I'm expecting to be met,' she said plaintively. 'Is this by any chance the — '

'That's the Norwich diligence, ma'am. Staying the night here.'

Deborah tried to remember the map she had studied before setting out. 'I would not have thought it too many miles to cover in an evening.'

'Not when the night's a clear one, no. But the way that wind do blow . . . ' The man shrugged. 'You're a stranger hereabouts, ma'am?'

'Yes.'

He shrugged again, as if that were answer enough. Deborah glanced back through the arch. There was no sign of any vehicle other than this dark abandoned one here.

'Nobody'll be venturing out on the brecks with things like this.' The ostler waved towards the pallid flickering light through a side window. 'Them as knows has booked in for the night, and them as is quick enough.'

It was inconceivable that here in her own country, in the brisk middle of the nineteenth century, her journey should grind to a halt so few miles from its goal. Deborah had single-handedly arranged cross-channel transport for her father, alive and dead; and now, in England of all places, had been halted in an alien wilderness.

The ostler glanced towards the bar, eager to go in and add to the companionable buzz within. 'Where was it you'd be wanting to go, anyway?'

'Toft Warren House.'

He stared at her. 'But that burned down these two nights ago.'

She was dizzy with tiredness and disbelief. 'Burned down? But ... what about Mr. and Mrs. Fleming?'

'They'd be the couple living there?'

'Of course they were! What happened? Where did they go when ... after it happened?'

'Didn't go nowhere, from all I hear.'

'I don't understand.'

'You've come a good way to see 'em, ma'am?' He appeared almost as dazed as she was.

'What happened to them?' she insisted.

'Well, from what's being told, they

neither of 'em got out. No way of getting help to 'em, not way out there in the middle of the breck.'

2

Deborah refused to accept it. Soon Beatrice would be there, apologising for being late, making nonsense of what this man had said. Her father's slow death had been inevitable; Beatrice's sudden one was unthinkable . . .

'Reckon you'd best be having a drink while you think it over.' The man's tone became sympathetic. 'Try the little snug on the right. Not so noisy there. I'll get the missus to sit in with you.'

Deborah took a hesitant step towards the door. Then she heard, borne on the wind, the clatter of hoofs and a rumble of wheels along the street. She turned and hurried out through the archway. Simultaneously the dark man appeared on the step of the inn, also staring demandingly across the station approach. Now, Deborah prayed, Beatrice must appear. The man's story would prove a fantasy, a grotesque mistake.

A brougham plastered with sand swung in beside the dim lights of the inn. Over his nose and mouth the coachman wore a scarf, which he tugged away as he jumped down. 'Sir Randall. Sorry to be late, sir. It's proper thick out there.'

'We can get back?'

'Yes, taking it easy, we'll fetch up all right.'

He swung the door open, and the dark man put one foot on the step. Then he glanced back at Deborah and the ostler, edging out of the gloom behind her. He jerked his head peremptorily. The ostler approached warily, head slightly lowered, not wanting to look him in the eye.

A question was barked, carried away from Deborah's ears by a swirl and scurry of grit-laden wind through the courtyard.

'Yes . . . Toft Warren . . . that's what she said, sir.'

Sir Randall's gaze snapped from the man to Deborah, confronted by some unwelcome decision. Then he came toward her.

'I understand, madam, that you have come in search of Toft Warren House.'

17

'That is so.'

'Alone?'

'I was expecting to be met.'

'You are, I take it, Mrs. Fleming's sister? The resemblance is striking.'

'Her half-sister. Deborah Ritchie.'

'Miss Ritchie.' He sketched a curt bow. 'My name is Gaunt. Randall Gaunt. I also gather that Johnson there has broken the news to you. Without much grace or tact, I'll be bound.'

'I still don't understand. It's not possible. I still don't . . . I can't . . . '

'This in an infernally draughty place for discussing such events. May I offer you accommodation for the night while you recover from the shock? Clearly you will need to revise whatever plans you had.'

He held his head rigid when he talked, and his voice was as stiff and level as his gaze. So far as she could judge he was a man in his early thirties but with the gravity of one much older. Not a man addicted to discussion: he expected a simple yes or no on any matter before him.

Deborah was confused. 'It's most kind of you, sir. But I have been accustomed to make my own dispositions. I shall speak to the landlord of the inn — '

'And he'll tell you it is full. And if it were not, it would still be hardly suitable for an unaccompanied young lady.' His fingers snapped a decision at the coachman. 'Critten, this lady's trunk. I fancy I saw it being put to one side in the station.'

'Sir, I really can't permit you to go to this trouble.'

'At my home you will find adequate staff. My housekeeper will offer any assistance you require. In the morning you're free to make alternative arrangements. Or to go back wherever you may have come from.' So far as Sir Randall Gaunt was concerned, the question was settled and he was impatient to be away.

'Why should you concern yourself with me?' asked Deborah.

'Because the whole thing is my concern, unfortunately. The house that has been burned down is my property, on

19

my land. The news has brought me back from London. Time I can ill afford. And a loss which I would not wish to afford.'

Deborah feebly tried a last protest. 'The ostler told me nothing could get across the . . . whatever it was he called it.'

'The breckland? My man knows his way and the prevailing conditions. He got here, he will get us safely back.'

Deborah reflected that the poor fellow would hardly dare do otherwise. Gaunt's firm hand was under her elbow. She stepped up and into the carriage.

The lights of the strung-out little town dropped away behind. Once beyond the shelter of the main street, the brougham was rocked and punched by the gusting wind.

Sir Randall sank deep into thought for several minutes. Then: 'My condolences on the death of Mrs. Fleming.'

'It's so hard to grasp. Beatrice . . . '

'At the moment I can offer little solace. I know as little as you do.'

Deborah nodded and looked away, freeing him from the duty of making conversation. She wondered what business it was that occupied him in London, and how inconvenient it might have been for him to tear himself away on hearing news of the fire.

Light spilled fitfully into the carriage. Somewhere beyond the drifting haze of sand the moon had risen. Clumps of bracken by the roadside were picked out in silver and then masked again. Skeletal groups of twisted pines jutted from the middle distance.

Sir Randall forced himself to be polite again. 'This must seem a strange region to someone so new to it.'

'I have had no chance to learn anything about it.'

Moonlight fell briefly upon his face. The severe line of nose and jaw was not softened by the close trim of his side whiskers. 'Some thousands of years ago — ' He had the terse, detached manner of a lecturer. ' — this was one of the most densely populated regions of Britain. The people dug flint from the chalk. There are ancient flint mines forty and fifty feet deep, lost in the scrub

— miles from anywhere we would now consider habitable. They even farmed in the brakes. But the sand in the chalk never lies still for long. Get a wind like this one tonight, and you get a sand-storm. Sand floods have drowned entire hamlets: which is why we have so few. It's a land for rough shooting. And rabbits. Nothing else.'

Deborah wondered why he lived here — or, at least, had property here — but sensed that there was little point in asking; sensed, also, that although he might have interests in London, he belonged here. His manner was the abrasive one of those undulating miles of sand and stone and stunted bushes she glimpsed through the window.

'The stage drivers rightly don't trust it,' he concluded. 'There's little sense in foundering halfway across with sand up to your axles.'

The carriage lurched as it crawled along, and the sound of sand spattering against the coachwork was as loud as the rumble of wheels. Then they turned left, and the pace quickened slightly.

'Another fifteen minutes,' said Gaunt. In his bones he must know every turn and twist of the rutted road. He sat back with his arms folded. They were silent for the rest of the journey.

Abruptly, as they passed between tall stone gateposts on to a gravelled drive, the moon raced out on an unexpected patch of clear sky. Deborah caught fragmentary impressions of a flint-grey house with saw-toothed battlements and an unidentifiable soaring pillar set to one side; and then the carriage jolted to a halt, and the door was being opened for her.

'Saxwold Hall, Miss Ritchie,' said Sir Randall. 'I think you will find it preferable to the Ingmere hostelry.'

The entrance hall struck chill the moment Deborah set foot in it. A fine ascending curve of highly polished stair-rail and a balustrade above; an old refectory table in the centre of the hall burnished like copper; a fine painting of a windmill in the Flemish style radiating tranquillity above the spread of warm-hued floor tiling — yet the place was cold and unresponsive. So might a room in the Sleeping Beauty's castle have looked: admirably appointed, but without a living pulse. A butler stood by the door through which Deborah had entered. The housekeeper, in a white cap and high-buttoned black dress with white collar, was crossing the floor from a door beneath the stairs.

'Welcome home, Sir Randall.'

'Thank you, Mrs. Thurton.'

The woman included Deborah in her curtsey, with a hint of query in the turn of her head.

'Mrs. Thurton, Miss Ritchie will be spending the night here. Possibly longer, if it will be of assistance to her.'

'I didn't know you'd be bringing a guest, sir.' It expressed the semi-humorous reproach of a favoured old retainer rather than genuine annoyance.

After Gaunt had explained her presence swiftly and dispassionately, Mrs. Thurton suggested the use of the guest room in the east wing. Gaunt nodded approval. Deborah's trunk and travelling bag were unobtrusively removed by a young man with a slight limp.

'I did light a fire in your room, sir, and also in the study. Whilst the young lady's room is warming, perhaps she may sit in the study?'

Again Gaunt nodded. 'I will send a glass of madeira in to warm you, Miss Ritchie. I shall not disturb you; I have a few things to attend to. We shall meet at dinner.'

Mrs. Thurton stood by Deborah's elbow. She was deferential and unhurried, but Deborah felt herself being directed: the housekeeper knew her master's routine and knew the exact place for everything and everybody. Incongruously, Deborah remembered her father's loyal, imperturbable batman.

She allowed herself to be guided into Sir Randall's richly panelled study. A fire was burning in the grate, and candle lamps had been set in brackets to either side of a large bookcase.

'Make yourself comfortable, miss. Won't be long until your room is ready.'

Mrs. Thurton showed her a wash-basin in a curtained corner recess. The young man with the limp brought a jug of hot water and towels. There was no looking-glass in the alcove. Nevertheless, Deborah was grateful. She washed away the stains of travel, and emerged from the curtains to find that an armchair had been set beside the fire, with a glass of wine on a table beside it. She sat down and tried to relax, looking about her.

The bookcase was filled with medical tomes. There were no pictures on the walls, but when she got up and walked towards a large flat-topped cabinet she found an anatomical chart spread out on it. Its colouring made her mildly queasy. She returned to her drink, and realised she was hungry.

Yet she didn't want to stay here, or to dine with Sir Randall and have to be obliged to him for his brusque, reluctant hospitality; but what else could she do? The wind moaned about the house. Deborah went to the window and pulled aside one of the heavy chenille curtains. She could just make out a blurred stretch of lawn, what might be a hedge or stone wall, and that strange pillar which from this angle looked like a tower with a pyramidal cap. She closed the curtains and turned back to the study, feeling more than ever lost.

Without warning, there came a thumping and rumbling that shuddered through every fibre of the building. Deborah had been about to sit down, but was still on her feet when Mrs. Thurton returned.

'Oh, gracious, did that startle you, miss? It's only the master starting up his steam-pump for the boiler room. We manage without it when he's not here: Boynton doesn't trust himself with it. But Sir Randall wants it for his bathroom. And,' said Mrs. Thurton importantly, 'for his laboratory, when he's working up there.'

'Laboratory?'

'Always at work.' The specialness of it had rubbed off on her. 'Experimenting, shutting himself away. The master can't bear to be unoccupied. Or,' she added, 'interrupted.'

The thudding died away to a faint throb.

'The fire in your room's going nicely,' Mrs. Thurton went on. 'Taken the chill off. If you're ready . . . '

The door was wide open. Mrs. Thurton held a candle above her head, leading the way without waiting for an answer. They went upstairs and along a draughty corridor of leaping shadows.

'Not that it's all that cold this time of year, but when a room hasn't been used in a long while . . . ' The room was in fact an attractive one, with Dutch tiles around the grate and a light flowered wallpaper. The bed cover and its valance were in pink and blue chintz. A mirror above the mantelpiece acted as a reflector to a quartet of candles in sconces.

'Thank you,' said Deborah.

'Dinner will be in half an hour,' said Mrs. Thurton, and left. In addition to the mirror, there was a pier glass in one corner beside a mahogany wardrobe. Changing, Deborah studied herself in it. She had been disconcerted by Sir Randall Gaunt's hazarding that she was Beatrice's sister. They both had red hair — an inheritance, their mother had said, from a dead grandfather — but whereas Beatrice's had been sandy, Deborah's hair was a deep auburn. Now, leaning towards the glass, she tried to see Beatrice's features. But Beatrice had a smaller mouth, and her eyes were forever bright and inquiring and restless. *Mine*, thought Deborah critically, *don't tell anybody anything. Except perhaps when I'm angry.*

She would never again see Beatrice. Never look into pale green eyes, never hear the irrepressible chatter from that mocking little rosebud mouth.

She went down to dinner in the plain but less austere dove-grey dress she had planned to wear on her first evening with Beatrice and her husband. Sir Randall sat facing her across a long table, with his back to a painting of a beautiful young woman. Dark-haired, pale-skinned, with white shoulders rising exquisitely from a froth of lace, the sitter had been caught by the artist in a smile she was charmingly trying to suppress: she was so vibrant that she seemed on the verge of leaning out of the frame.

They were served with partridge. After a couple of mouthfuls, Sir Randall raised one eyebrow to invite her approval. She was glad to give it.

'Boynton, to whom are we indebted for these?'

'They were sent over by Mr. Fleming a week ago, sir, after his first shoot of the season. I gather he was not sure of your whereabouts, but had achieved such a remarkable bag that he was distributing the results lavishly. Poor young gentleman. He was in rare form, by all accounts.'

Deborah laid her fork down.

Sir Randall's high cheekbones tautened. 'Miss Ritchie, on Boynton's behalf I do apologise for the introduction of what I know is a painful subject. He was ignorant of the relationship. It was thoughtless of me to come out with the question in the first place.'

The butler began to make a bewildered apology, but Gaunt waved him down. Pouring claret into their glasses with a shaky hand, Boynton shot a glance at his employer and hurried from the room.

'As you observed,' said Deborah, 'he had no reason to know who I was ... unless Mrs. Thurton — but no, I don't imagine she's quick to gossip.'

'None of my servants gossip.'

She ventured: 'You said that the house where Mr. Fleming and Beatrice lived was on your land.'

'I spend much of my time in London. The smaller house, Toft Warren, was little more than a shooting lodge for my ancestors. Of little use to me. I let the house and shooting rights to Edwin Fleming and his wife. Glad to have someone making use of the land.'

The provocative quirk of a smile drew her gaze back to the painting. 'Your wife also lives in London?'

He reached for his glass, drank, and said: 'My wife has been dead for nine years and five weeks.' It was clear that he wanted no condolences. 'And you . . . ' Adroitly he steered the conversation away. 'I don't recall your half-sister speaking of you. Not that we met very often.'

Deborah found it calming in a way, to talk to someone so impersonal in his attitude. She explained that her father had married late in life, the young widow of a brother officer killed in the fighting at

Rangoon. The new Mrs. Ritchie had one daughter, Beatrice, nine months old at the time of the wedding.

'And was shortly to have another?' Gaunt prompted.

'Within a year of the marriage.'

'You and your half-sister got on well together?'

'There was no reason why we should not.' Her father had always been scrupulously fair towards his step-daughter; and Deborah had always abided by her father's standards.

'A most attractive young woman,' observed Gaunt, 'though a trifle erratic.'

'Erratic?' It was just the word Deborah herself would have chosen, but she felt defensive on Beatrice's behalf. 'She was impulsive, certainly. But so very much alive.'

A footman came in to remove their plates, and returned with a bowl of fresh fruit.

Deborah said: 'I know so little of their life here. You saw a great deal of them?'

'They visited a few times during their first months in the neighbourhood. I gave a dinner party or two. But — ' His tone hinted at a rift or at least a cooling of friendship. ' — I haven't seen Mrs. Fleming for more than a year now. Or Mr. Fleming. I spend much of my time in London.'

'I never met Edwin. When our mother died, Beatrice came into money left in trust by her father. It was only a few days from her twenty-first birthday. She married shortly after that.'

'With your father's approval?'

Deborah sliced a peach. It had been typical of Beatrice, she silently recollected, that the whole affair should have been rushed through so thoughtlessly. Colonel Ritchie had gone off with his regiment, Deborah was back at school for her finishing year — and neither of them was given an opportunity to meet the bridegroom or attend the ceremony. Aloud she said: 'My father knew of Edwin's father, General Fleming. It was an admirable match. But just as the wedding was taking place, my father was injured in battle and then almost died from sickness afterwards.'

'Severe injuries?'

Gaunt showed an awakening technical interest and asked a number of searching questions which, thought Deborah sadly, might better have been asked by one of the few surgeons on the scene of the disaster. Colonel Ritchie had been shot twice in the left leg, and had the kneecap shattered while fighting the Sikhs at Ferozeshah. There was no field hospital, and although two harassed surgeons did what they could in the terrible aftermath of the battle, it was a makeshift treatment. Some fevered casualties, including Colonel Ritchie, drank from a well contaminated by the Sikhs with gunpowder and the corpses of men and horses. Only a handful survived; and Colonel Ritchie never fully recovered. It was the damage done to his stomach and intestines, rather than the hideous leg wounds, that drove him to one source of healing after another, one European spa after another.

Deborah awoke to the fact that her host was studying her with a more keenly personal interest than before. But it was with academic rather than prying curiosity that he asked: 'And I trust you, too, inherited a worthy subsistence? Nothing for Beatrice this time?'

Deborah said bluntly: 'My father was always fair. Beatrice had been well provided for by her own father, so he did not leave her as much as he left me. But there is a sufficiency. Or would have been.'

Belated acceptance that Beatrice really must be dead, added to the accumulated tiredness of the long day and the wine she had drunk, brought her perilously close to tears. Choking them back, she said at random: 'Whatever happened to my telegraph message?'

'The post office at the Stannard Arms provides daily incoming and outgoing mail and telegraph services. Provided the road to Ingmere is passable. And provided the publican's aunt isn't out gleaning or skinning coneys. She may have tried to send a message back to you; or may have tucked your communication away in a drawer, having not the slightest idea what to do with it.'

His analysis was probably as accurate as it was heartless. Deborah wished to say or hear nothing further.

Gaunt took a gold hunter from his waistcoat and flipped it open. 'If you wish to retire, Miss Ritchie, please don't let me detain you. I still have much to occupy me.' As they got up, he added: 'In the morning, perhaps we may both go to inspect the scene of the tragedy and make the necessary inquiries. I am sure you are as anxious to have the whole dismal business settled as I am.'

She hoped she would be capable of assessing it as coolly as he undoubtedly would.

* * *

Deborah lay awake a long time, tossing and turning as the dying firelight smudged the wall. There was still so much to be explained. Just like Beatrice, the suddenness and clumsiness of it! Deborah began to accuse the face that swirled at her through a half-dream, a hurricane of whirling sand; then jerked awake with a pounding in her breast and the frightening awareness of Beatrice very close, on the point of telling her something terribly urgent, terribly important.

Darkness rolled in on her. When her eyelids closed, fire burned red through them. Somewhere a house was burning. And Beatrice clawed a way out of the flames towards her.

Then a silver streak of daylight. She opened her eyes, wondering what further trick of imagination this was, and found the earliest hint of dawn pencilled down one side of the window. She got out of bed and drew back the curtain. The storm had died away. The landscape remained dusty with shadow, the dark lawn dropping away from dark terraced levels towards a flint-pebbled wall. Beyond was the endless heath.

There was a flicker of movement beside some stunted bushes. Deborah watched as a flimsy ghost materialised from the foliage and flitted with an oddly twisted motion towards the building. The figure was that of a girl, her left arm crooked at an uncomfortable angle across her stomach. She stopped for a moment, her face touched by the dawn as she looked up at the length of the house, seeming to sense that she was being watched. Deborah stepped back from the window. Somewhere below she heard the click of a door opening and closing, followed by the faintest tap of footsteps on a staircase that must run up the far end of this wing.

Some serving girl scurrying back to her garret from an assignation? The idea of a lovers' meeting in a storm-ridden night out on the breck seemed incongruous. But then, everything she had so far encountered in this desolate land was incongruous.

Deborah got back into bed but was unable to sleep as the light strengthened and flooded into the room. She heard no further sounds until in some yard there was the clatter of a pail, and somewhere a window opened and there was a brief chatter of voices.

Frozen on her mind was the picture of that girl's face, the way she had momentarily held her head when afraid of being observed, the twisted arm and twisted expression: a picture of pain and desperation.

3

The gutted shell of Toft Warren House was still faintly smoking. Its acrid smell drifted across to the coach as Deborah got down. A scattering of smuts, blown along the lane by yesterday's storm, fidgeted now like black insects disturbed by the faintest of breezes. Sir Randall took Deborah's arm to help her across a stony patch of dusty ground.

All that remained of what must have been a stylish little Jacobean pavilion, converted into a trim two-storey house, was a jagged brick outline. Sand had already settled on the scorched bricks, and on the ashes of collapsed timbering inside.

'Too much wood,' grunted Sir Randall as they stopped within the pathetic remnant of a doorway. 'My grandfather's fault. He spent prodigally — oak from Sherwood and Sussex, Scandinavian softwoods shipped in through King's

Lynn, to make over the whole interior. Panelling, staircases, window seats — all superb. But once let it catch fire . . . '

Somebody moved in another black-toothed gap. When he caught sight of them he tramped across the rubble, his boots kicking up gouts of dark powder.

'My bailiff.' Even before the man reached them, Sir Randall was snapping out: 'Well, Runnacre? Any explanation for all this?'

The bailiff tipped his hat respectfully at Deborah. His face was a deep russet hue after years of having been flailed by whips of wind and sand.

'It's hard to tell, sir. There was nobody here but Mr. and Mrs. Fleming. Nobody saw a thing, except for the flames in the sky from a long way off.'

'Nobody? What about the servants?'

'They had all been dismissed some weeks earlier, sir. Towards the end there was only old Mrs. Pigle from Meddle-heath, a warrener's widow. Hardly the sort to keep the place in good order.'

'And where was this Mrs. Pigle on the

night of the fire?' Gaunt was ominously quiet.

'She, too, had left. A couple of days before.'

'The house was let with strict provisos about its adequate maintenance. Why were these not observed?'

'There were rumours of Mr. Fleming being in financial difficulties. The village grocer, and the gunsmith in Ingmere — both spoke to me of unpaid bills.'

'And what did you do about it?'

'On two occasions I raised the subject with Mr. Fleming himself. He was extremely aggressive, sir. He assured me that he would pay in his own good time, and that when you returned he would ask you to instruct me that spying was not one of my duties.'

'Did he, indeed? You should have notified me.'

'I thought it could wait until your next visit, sir. I didn't want to drag you back from London for something that might have settled itself by the time — '

'It has settled itself,' said Gaunt, 'and I

42

have been dragged back from London as a result.'

'I'm sorry, sir.'

'But Beatrice!' exclaimed Deborah. 'My sister — '

'I'm sorry, miss, I'd no idea.'

'Did she . . . were they . . . '

Runnacre said: 'It seemed to me, miss . . . sir, that Mr. Fleming had been drinking heavily. Struck me that way when I was asking about the staff, and his bills. And the drink itself, that was another bill he ran up a tidy amount, so I learned yesterday. Looks like they were nigh penniless. Maybe that's why, if they were a bit desperate — '

'That's enough.' Sir Randall cut him short.

Not a penny between them? The tragedy that Deborah had last night forced herself to accept was now, in daylight, growing even less credible. How could Edwin and Beatrice have run through Beatrice's inheritance, on top of whatever Edwin had brought to the marriage, in such a short time?

The two men stepped down into the

mess left by the blaze. Sir Randall picked up a sliver of charred wood, crumbling it between his fingers. 'It must have been a veritable furnace in here.' His gaze raked the upper courses of the remaining brickwork.

'Good job the walls contained it,' said the bailiff. 'If the bracken had caught, the wind would have fanned a right old fire across the heath.' He ran his fingertips along a few inches of wall and examined their blackness. 'A furnace, that's just what it was . . . with all this wood in here, and then the logs and the peat store as well. Oh, and that's another one: the carter who brought the peat in off the marshland didn't get paid.'

'Let me have a list of outstanding debts.'

'I should like a copy, also,' said Deborah firmly.

Sir Randall's sharp glance indicated a likelihood of his arguing the point. Instead, after a moment's reflection, he drew his bailiff farther into the debris and spoke in an undertone.

'Remains . . . bones . . . ?'

Deborah gulped and turned away, to stare across the breck.

'Pretty well incinerated,' said Runnacre. He went on in a lower tone: 'Coroner . . . Doctor Abbott . . . '

'Old nincompoop.'

A few yards away, between Deborah and the coach, a torn scrap of muslin, singed along one edge, fluttered then caught on a large piece of flint. How many more pitiful mementoes had been snatched out by the wind and tossed on to the uncaring wilderness?

The men were returning, Runnacre saying: 'Left my nag tethered on the other side, sir. I'll meet you in Meddleheath.'

As the coach lurched along the track to a junction with a narrow road, Gaunt leaned back with an explosive sigh.

'Confounded untidy, the whole sorry business.'

'I should like a copy,' Deborah repeated, 'of the list you mentioned.'

'That's not necessary. My responsibility entirely. I accepted young Fleming's references, and his word. So I make myself responsible for the outcome.'

'If there are debts, I'm sure we'll find that they can be met out of the estate. I simply don't believe that all Beatrice's money can have disappeared.'

'Don't you?' The cynical twist of his lips infuriated her. 'I think you should make up your mind to believe it, and let us clear up the loose ends as swiftly as may be. As next of kin, you must have financial and other matters that will now need attention. Fortunate for you that your father's legacy to Mrs. Fleming did not have time to reach her, otherwise it would have gone the way of the rest. I presume it will now come to you. I'm sure you will make more sober use of it.'

Deborah tensed. It had not occurred to her to start calculating already what changes might take place in her own circumstances. She said challengingly: 'First I would like to know the full story.'

'I doubt if we shall ever know that,' Gaunt said brusquely: 'You must forgive my apparent callousness, Miss Ritchie. I have seen many deaths and much suffering. I find it easier to treat them all as everyday inconveniences, to be dealt with rationally and disposed of in the shortest possible time.'

Deborah could not be so methodical with her emotions. As the carriage rolled on its way, she wrestled with the new confusions aroused by the tale of unpaid bills, servants sent away, and Edwin's heavy drinking. What had gone wrong with their finances — or with the marriage itself?

The road began to curve over a slight rise. A church tower came in view, drawing them very slowly towards it.

Sir Randall broke the silence. 'You wish to accompany me when I call upon the coroner?'

'I hadn't thought about it. If there's anything he can tell me — '

'I doubt that. An elderly physician, and never a very observant one. We shall all be as wise at the end of his inquest as we were at the beginning. Are you intending,' he demanded, 'to ask for a full formal investigation?'

Instinctively she wanted to do whatever Sir Randall Gaunt would advocate her not doing. But whatever an inquest uncovered, it would not alter the basic, unavoidable verdict. The two were dead. 'You're quite sure,' she accused him, 'that nobody is ever going to tell me anything?'

'I haven't quite put it in those words. You'll find many tongues to tell you any number of things.' Gaunt peered out of the window. They were slowing past the churchyard lychgate. 'With so few diversions hereabouts, the local inhabitants always have a great many colourful tales to tell, greatly embroidered. And every one different!'

★   ★   ★

Meddleheath consisted of one rutted street and two back lanes. The northern side of the street was made up of three terraces of flint cottages. Facing them, the church was too large for its neighbours and had obviously been neglected over many years. The thatch was tearing away down a slope of the roof, and a crude wooden buttress had been rammed against a crack in the north wall. Part of the churchyard was waist-high in coarse grass. Gravestones tilted drunkenly, their lettering eaten away or slimed by fungus.

A tall young man strode down the path as the carriage halted, carrying a scythe that he propped against the wall before opening the gate to his visitors. He ran his left forefinger under his clerical collar, and mopped his brow.

'Ormesby, isn't it?' Gaunt greeted him.

'You have a good memory, Sir Randall.'

'Considering that I've attended your church only once during your incumbency?' Gaunt allowed himself a thin smile. 'Miss Ritchie, this is the Reverend Gerald Ormesby, rector of this parish.'

'Miss Ritchie.' The rector's muscular grip clamped around her hand, while he stared into her eyes and gave her a broad smile. She had met his kind before: one of the eager new evangelicals, seething with plans for reform and the revitalising of their church.

Gaunt said: 'Miss Ritchie is the late Mrs. Fleming's sister. She arrived late yesterday.'

Ormesby's smile transformed into one of deep condolence, without any loss of sincerity. 'My dear Miss Ritchie, I regret you have had to pay your first visit to us on such a sad occasion. If I can offer any comfort — '

'You can,' said Gaunt. 'I consider it preferable for Miss Ritchie to stay here while I have a few words with old Abbott. There's no reason why she should have to endure him on top of everything else.'

The rector glanced uncertainly at Deborah. Sir Randall added more gently: 'The decision is entirely yours, Miss Ritchie. But I do beg you to let me speak to the coroner alone. If he has anything to communicate that may be of personal concern to you, I promise to fetch you. Will you rely on me?'

Deborah had long prided herself on being competent, on needing no help in making decisions. But with her father's death and these other deaths hard upon it, the overwound spring must have snapped. Let Gaunt take over, let him be as harsh and short and matter-of-fact as he chose.

'I shall be most grateful,' she said.

'I shall not keep you long.'

Mr. Ormesby was boyishly delighted to have her in his charge for a little while. He was full of plans for renovating the fabric and the congregation. It was hard to imagine where he would find enough people out of the brecks to fill even a handful of his pews, but there was no denying his determination. He led Deborah through the old stone porch into the dank nave, while he pointed out faults which could still, before it was too late, be restored to their original beauty.

Ormesby took her to inspect the damage inflicted by Cromwell's image-smashers on the font two centuries ago. The desecration was still real and immediate to him. Plaster was coming away from the chancel arch in papery segments and solid lumps. Fragments of a wooden lectern were heaped into the corner of a box pew.

'Beetle, I'm afraid. The wooden plinth was eaten right through, and when it gave way, the whole lectern collapsed and splintered into several pieces.'

'Mr. Ormesby, were my sister and her

husband regular members of your congregation?'

'I've been here only seven or eight months,' he said apologetically. 'I was told they had been somewhat irregular communicants, and though I did venture to call on Mr. and Mrs. Fleming, they showed little inclination to travel such distances each Sunday.'

'Would you have any objection to their being buried here?'

'Assuredly not, if that is what you wish.'

Words seemed to come out of their own accord. 'We might consider some suitable memorial for Beatrice and Edwin. Something which would fit in with your plans for the church.'

'That's most generous of you, Miss Ritchie. But . . . no, you mustn't make a decision now.' Afraid of being too eager, Ormesby backed away with an endearing shyness. 'Please. Do give it more thought, and of course if you decide . . . but I think I should leave you to meditate on it . . . ' He bumped his way off into the vestry.

Deborah, after another survey of the

decaying interior, went out and strolled slowly round the churchyard.

A stooped figure came in through the lychgate, an old woman carrying a shabby straw basket. Without noticing Deborah, she shuffled over the grass to one of the few graves which gave any sign of being regularly tended. The basket thumped heavily to the ground. As Deborah watched, the woman took out a large flint and laid it at one corner of the grave. Three times more she plunged her hand into the basket, and three more flints were set at the other three corners.

Deborah stepped forward. At the rustle of her feet, the old woman looked up and gave a little start.

'Good morning,' said Deborah. There was no response. She made slowly for the path, but stopped to look at the nearest of the newly placed stones. It was a large flint in the shape of a roughly squashed oval; and through it had been worn a wide hole. She could not resist asking: 'Are the others the same?' A glance confirmed that they were. Not all quite the same shape, but all with a hole driven right through.

'Eye stones,' mumbled the woman. 'Lucky stones, to keep evil away.'

'Oh. I see.'

'Do you, miss?' A seedy chuckle rasped out of the old throat. 'Better than stones with names on. Especially when you can't be sure if the names has a right to be there.'

Deborah could not fathom what this meant. But the talk of names drew her attention to the lettering on the head-stone of this grave, carved only two years previously. It declared that Charles Pigle was not lost but gone before.

'Mrs. Pigle? Do you have any connec-tion with the Mrs. Pigle who worked at Toft Warren House? My sister and brother-in-law, Mr. and Mrs. Fleming, engaged someone of that name.'

'Ah. So that's who you'd be.' The woman rose stiffly. 'You're staying in the village, then?'

'Sir Randall Gaunt has been kind enough to offer me hospitality for a few days.'

'Has he, now?' The palsied head cocked slyly to one side. 'Best mind your step, miss. Many a one's gone into that place and . . . well, who's to say?'

'What are you trying to tell me?'

'Not for me to say, miss.' Slyness gave way to wariness. But she could not subdue her tongue.

'No getting round it, though. What with his wife dying the way she did, and him there forcing it on till there was no life left in her, poor soul — and not satisfied but what he has to go *on* cutting folk up. Call himself a surgeon? Butcher, more like. And something worse. And as for that sister of yours, that Mrs. Fleming, if you ask me . . . ' The strident tone sank to a mumble.

'Yes?' Deborah challenged.

There was a little snigger. 'You'd be paying off some of what they owed?'

'If there are any genuine amounts outstanding, I'm prepared to consider settling.'

'Oh, they're genuine enough. One reason why I left.'

'So *you're* the Mrs. Pigle.'

'Never said I wasn't. Not that the money was the only reason I left, mind. Worked for them as long as I could in spite of everything. Him and his drink and his language and everything. Gave my best — no one can say I didn't. Till I couldn't stand it no more.'

Things must undoubtedly have been bad with Edwin and Beatrice if even an old slattern like this could endure them no longer.

Deborah said: 'You weren't there when the fire broke out.'

'No, that I weren't. And not the only one to be gone by then.'

'The other servants — '

Mrs. Pigle snorted, 'They were gone long before she'd be bothered with the likes of me. No, I'm not talking about them being off. I'm talking about her.'

Deborah held her breath.

'High time *somebody* paid up.' It came out in a rush. 'And better that, paying up, than wasting money on tombstones if that's what you had in mind. Or a stone with more than the one name on it, anyway. Because you couldn't honestly be sure, not the way I see it.'

'What do you mean?' Deborah prompted.

'Who says your Mrs. Fleming was ever in that fire, then? She weren't in the house all week before it happened. Leastways, not while I was there. Just him. Out shooting every day, killing just for the sake of killing, and then bidding fair to kill himself with drink every night. And what kind of spell was *she* under, to go off like that?'

'Where did she go?'

'I don't know, that's a fact. And all I'm saying is she weren't back by the time I left. Who's to say she ever did come back?'

4

The churchyard gate squealed on its hinges. Sunlight struck down through the crocketed pinnacles of the tower upon the flaxen hair of a young man whose gaze was set on Deborah. Alongside him was a slim girl perhaps a few years younger than he, though they might have been twins: both were fair, had the same patrician nose, finely arrogant chin, and the same leisurely self-assurance. She wore a riding habit; he had a short impeccably cut frock-coat with a bright blue stock, and carried a small ivory-handled whip.

Mrs. Pigle grabbed her basket and scuttled away round the east end of the church.

The young man chuckled. 'What mischief has that old crone been up to?'

His wide eyes were a startling gentian blue. Here, too, the girl echoed him, though hers betrayed a shyness that belied the autocratic set of her head. They could well be descendants of those Vikings who had ravaged the area centuries ago, shedding blood and then mingling their blood with that of the East Anglians.

'I'm sure that I am addressing Deborah.' His voice was as fervent as his eyes.

Taken aback by his familiarity, Deborah murmured, 'Deborah Ritchie, yes.'

'So we've found you at last.' He smiled at his companion and she was quick to smile back.

'I didn't know that anyone was searching for me.'

'But we've been extremely worried about you. I scarcely slept last night. Having failed to collect you from Ingmere, I couldn't rest until we set out in pursuit this morning.'

'You came to meet me at Ingmere?'

'Regrettably, no. It was our intention to do so, but the storm on the breck defeated us.'

'You knew, then, that I would be arriving at the station.'

'Forgive me.' His head bowed. 'My name is Stannard. Justin Stannard. This is my sister, Isabel. And we have also established that you are Miss Deborah Ritchie.' They shook hands. His heartiness reminded her of the Reverend Gerald Ormesby's, but there was something more purposeful behind it. Briefly hushed as he commiserated with her over Beatrice's death, his voice soon rose irrepressibly again. 'Edwin and Beatrice were friends of ours. That is how we shall remember them, though in recent months we didn't meet as often as I'd have wished. But I must confess that the existence of such a beautiful sister was never revealed to me.'

'Beatrice did tell me she had a half-sister,' said Isabel Stannard. 'It had slipped my mind until your telegram came, and then when I mentioned it to Justin we guessed — '

'Miss Ritchie is worth more than a *mention*. She should have been invited to visit these parts long ago.'

Deborah said: 'You spoke of my telegram. It came into your hands, then?'

'I was perplexed at the time, when our postmistress came to me in a fine state.

Who was this Deborah?' His laugh bubbled up again. 'Yesterday you were only a name at the foot of a message. Now . . . '

'The postmistress brought it to *you*?

'My brother is, among other boring things, justice of the peace.'

'Petty sessions every other Thursday, in the back room of the Stannard Arms.' A self-deprecating flick of the wrist, and Stannard went on: 'Unable to prevent your journey, Miss Ritchie, we decided to meet you at the station and break the news to you as gently as possible. The storm turned us back. We could only hope that you would have found accommodation at the inn — dismal as the place is — and that we could reach you there this morning. We were on our way to do, taking this detour because the road is still blocked. A happy chance that we did so!'

'Sir Randall Gaunt's coachman succeeded in getting through last night,' Deborah ventured.

The blue of his eyes darkened as if a cloud had blotted out the sun. His sister said quickly: 'Saxwold Hall lies in a different direction, at a different angle of the wind, from the Priory.'

'And Gaunt would not scruple to risk the life of his coachman — or his guest.'

Beyond them and beyond the gate, Deborah saw Sir Randall stride out of the narrow lane and across the village street. His tread slackened when he saw that Deborah was not alone; then he came on again, more smartly than before.

'Lord Stannard. Miss Stannard.'

'Good day to you, Gaunt.'

'Sir Randall.' The girl's whisper was barely audible.

Deborah felt a prickling of embarrassment. Twice she had been about to address the young man as 'Mr. Stannard' and had been prevented only by the unquenchable flow of his talk.

Isabel Stannard had turned her head away from Sir Randall and flushed deeply, at the same time looking awkward and unhappy.

Sir Randall wasted no further time on formalities. 'That doddering old doctor,' he rapped out, 'incapable of committing himself. Waiting to be told to sign the death certificate, and told what the coroner's verdict ought to be.'

'In matters of life and death,' said Lord Stannard caustically, 'there's a lot to be said for not bungling one's diagnosis.'

The two men bristled at each other. Isabel laid long, slender fingers on her brother's arm.

Gaunt said: 'Since the fellow has no critical or scientific faculties of his own, would it be too much to ask what instructions you propose to give him?'

'It would scarcely be proper for me to influence the coroner in the conduct of his office.'

'Without such influence, he will conduct nothing at all.'

'My dear Gaunt, proper procedures must surely be observed, if only for Miss Ritchie's sake.'

'For Miss Ritchie's sake,' Gaunt said, matching his tone to Lord Stannard's, 'the happiest conclusion would be one which enabled her to return home without delay to settle her affairs, which cannot but be greatly complicated by these misfortunes.'

'Undoubtedly. But,' said Stannard airily, 'let her not be hurried away with any complications still unresolved.'

Unresolved complications? On the tip of Deborah's tongue was the name of Mrs. Pigle. Before she could tell them of the baffling doubt which the old woman had raised, Stannard went on: 'If it were not ungallant to take advantage of these unhappy circumstances, I'd go so far as to *prevent* our charming visitor hurrying away.'

His sister seemed to know intuitively what was expected of her. 'Miss Ritchie, if we could prevail on you to stay with us until you have satisfied yourself — '

'Miss Ritchie is already my guest,' said Randall Gaunt curtly. 'She is welcome to continue her stay until matters are settled and the funeral can take place.'

Stannard parried. 'But you are on your own, my dear fellow. At the Priory there will not merely be Isabel as company for Miss Ritchie, but also my mother.'

'It will be more seemly,' ventured Isabel.

'I return to London tomorrow to conclude business in which I was interrupted. There will be nothing unseemly in Miss Ritchie's remaining in my house.'

Such rivalry might have flattered Deborah if she had not sensed that she was merely a pawn in an old contest. 'You're very kind, all of you. What I most want, frankly, is to return to Edinburgh as soon as that can reasonably be arranged. As Sir Randall came to my rescue and took me in, and my luggage is still at Saxwold Hall, it seems sensible to return there. I would hope, though, not to be a burden on the household for one moment longer than circumstances dictate.'

Lord Stannard accepted her decision with a slow courteous nod. Yet the moment she had spoken, Deborah felt an inexplicable regret. Her words had halted his advance towards her. And that was as it should be. How could she possibly allow herself to feel this deplorable, turbulent desire that the two of them should draw closer instead of formally backing away? On such a short acquaintance it was certainly not seemly.

As they shook hands, Justin Stannard said: We shall meet again, Miss Ritchie. Very soon.'

★ ★ ★

Randall Gaunt was taciturn during the journey back to Saxwold Hall. Once, when Deborah glanced at him, she saw his brows drawn into a tight line, and one fist clenched painfully on his knee, and wondered what sudden thought or sharp physical anguish could have racked him so.

Only as they approached the gates of his home did he speak out. 'I trust you'll be guided by me, Miss Ritchie, and keep your distance from the Stannards.'

'Surely such an eminent, and eminently respectable family — '

'Powerful. Not necessarily the same thing as respectable. Do understand, Miss Ritchie: I know this region much better than you.'

'Respectability, so called, may perhaps

be too much in fashion nowadays. Strength is not to be despised.' She was not prepared to submit meekly to his high-handedness.

'You've had to shoulder a great many responsibilities for a young woman, and I admire your courage. But don't be too proud of your independence. It could be dangerous. Don't be too arbitrary in your decisions — in rejecting advice for the sake of rejecting it.'

'I thank you for your advice, then,' said Deborah as coolly as she could manage, 'and I shall bear it in mind.'

As she descended from the carriage, she saw the full spread of the house. Even in daylight it was sombre, its walls compacted from the eternal, inescapable local flint. It could have been fifty years old or five hundred. Two huge twisted chimneys thrust up from a battlemented roof. The buttressed porch might almost have been a defensive gatehouse. The proportions of the house were noble, but were those of a fortress rather than a home, grey and solid and defiant in the incongruously green lawns watered by a little stream which curved through the grounds. Only one striking splash of colour coaxed the eye away from the massive hulk of the house: the red brick tower between the stream and the outbuildings to the north.

Gaunt anticipated her unspoken question: 'A water tower. Supplies the engine and boiler-room.'

That evening they dined together again, under the tantalising smile of his lovely dead wife. Was it still, after so many years, the pain of her loss that lanced spasmodically through him?

During the meal he questioned Deborah about her experiences in France and Austria and elsewhere, making some shrewd observations on parts of Edinburgh with which he was familiar. He was a dutiful host but a distant one.

Deborah imagined, against her will, Justin Stannard sitting across the table from her. Then she banished the fantasy. It was shocking that she should have allowed herself to admit the vividness of its colours.

A maid tiptoed into the room behind a

footman and awaited instructions to remove plates. Deborah glanced at her, as she had glanced at two other girls in the corridors since her return from the village. None of them bore any resemblance to that spellbound wraith she had seen fluttering towards the house in the silver dawn.

As soon as dinner was ended, Gaunt said he was sure she would be glad of time to herself to consider what she had learned and what she wished to do. He would not intrude on her thoughts.

She wondered who, or what, waited for him somewhere else in the house.

Left alone, she tried to do what he had expected of her. But her brain refused to function. The impossible Mrs. Pigle kept muttering out of a swirling fog. Justin Stannard swaggered in and out. Terrible visions of Beatrice burning in her death agonies made a fiery whirlpool before her eyes; and were dissolved again by Mrs. Pigle's sly, incomprehensible hints.

In the morning Sir Randall repeated his invitation to her to stay as long as she wished. Then, as though partly retracting, he added: 'If you're anxious to be away, however, I suggest you set a date of departure and make sure it's clearly understood by Abbott and Stannard. Once they see you're in earnest, they'll be quick enough to dispose of their petty formalities. You can have the funeral, and that will be an end to it. Refuse to accept any deliberate prevarication.'

'Deliberate?'

'It's plain enough that Stannard would be prepared to draw out the proceedings for an excuse to keep you in the neighbourhood.'

'You flatter me.'

'No.' The word was strangely muted. He gave her a searching look, confirming some personal diagnosis. She felt he was indeed seeing her as a person for the first time since their encounter at Ingmere station. Now he was unsure of himself — or of her. Abruptly he snapped: 'It's no flattery to be seen as the prey of such a rake.' The rasp of it had almost the sound of jealousy. He paused. 'But I must lecture you no further, Miss Ritchie. It might have the opposite effect to that which I desire.' He held out his hand, dry and cold. 'But please be assured not only that you are at liberty to use Saxwold Hall for as long as it suits you, but that I earnestly wish you to do so. And then I wish you a safe return to your home — and recommend that you forget the sorrows of the breckland.'

There could hardly have been a greater contrast with Justin Stannard's hand-clasp and the invitation in his words and tone of voice.

When Gaunt had left, Deborah strolled through the grounds. The lawns were well trimmed and the few flower beds tended well enough, but in some way they lacked echoes, and reflected no light. Nobody ever came to saunter through them and praise them, so they had lost the ability to respond.

Deborah felt herself an exile in a foreign land.

The legal formalities must surely be tidied up in a rational way before long. There must be a decent funeral. There must be someone she could talk to, someone she could urge into action.

Again Mrs. Pigle taunted her from a distance. The old woman must be made to say more and to say it clearly. Yet in any serious inquiry it was more than likely that the legal solemnities would scare her off into silence and denial.

Deborah walked by the stream. It was little more than a trickle, though the depth of the bed suggested it normally ran higher. The parched yellow of the grass farther back from the bank gave evidence of a dry spell.

There was no sound save for an occasional rustle in the scratchy grass and that of Deborah's footsteps. Then the cry of a plover fell plaintively across the sky towards the dusty horizon.

In the middle of the morning, a chinking sound intruded. Deborah turned to find Mrs. Thurton bearing down on her with a bunch of keys ringing and swinging at her belt.

'There's a young lady to see you, miss. The Honourable Miss Stannard.'

A lady's phaeton stood in the drive with its folding cover up. Isabel Stannard had been shown into the small drawing-room and was waiting there with her back to the window. Her long, slender fingers were cool and slightly moist to the touch. She had come, she said without delay, to invite Miss Ritchie to lunch at Stannard Priory.

Deborah fought down an immediate desire to accept. 'I fancy Mrs. Thurton is expecting me to lunch here. She will already have made preparations.'

'I will speak to Mrs. Thurton.' On such ground Isabel was as sure of her authority as her haughty bearing suggested.

'It is most kind of you to call,' Deborah hedged. 'But really, I'm not sure — '

'You must come. Please. It would mean so much to my brother.' Then, hastily: 'To all of us, of course. My mother is especially anxious to meet you.'

It could do no harm to lunch with the Stannards. She would spend a couple of pleasant hours with them, and return to Saxwold Hall later in the day to continue her fruitless speculations.

Sir Randall Gaunt would not have approved. The mere thought of his displeasure sparked off rebellion in Deborah. She heard herself accepting, and saw not just pleasure but relief in the girl's face.

'While you're getting ready,' Isabel said gaily, 'I'll deal with Mrs. Thurton. Leave her to me. I've known her for ages.'

As they crossed the hall, Deborah noticed that the dining-room door was open. Framed in the opening was the picture on the far wall. She slowed; and the girl, too, slowed her pace and looked in.

'Did you ever meet Lady Gaunt?' Deborah asked.

'I was too young to come visiting then.'

'She cannot have been very old herself when she died. It was . . . sudden?'

'It was terrible.' Isabel shivered. 'Or so they said. But then, so many things were said, and . . . no, I'm sure they were all distorted. Justin has always been so extreme — he . . . ' She broke off. 'But I'm delaying you. Let's be away, shall we? It will all be much more cheerful when we're out of this house.'

Deborah went upstairs. She chose the

cabochon earrings she had been left, along with three other pairs, by her mother; but in her haste let one slip through her fingers. It bounced from the edge of the dressing-table to the floor, and lodged in a crack between two boards. Deborah stooped to prise it out.

The gap widened towards the wall, and close to the skirting-board she could see that something else had gone in even deeper. With one finger she eased it up, and managed to pull it clear.

She recognised it at once, and with good reason: she had chosen it herself. It was her father's last birthday present to Beatrice, sent as a matter of polite ritual and selected for him by Deborah. It was a small brooch with a setting of Bohemian garnets, bought in a village a few miles from Marienbad.

That was less than six months ago. Yet surely she remembered Sir Randall saying, on the evening of her arrival, that Beatrice had not visited Saxwold Hall during the last year?

Deborah put the brooch thoughtfully

into the bottom of her reticule. Deep down, she was sure she had made no mistake.

5

The first sight of Stannard Priory was a pleasurable shock. The drive had taken just under an hour, along unhedged and unfenced ribbons of road marred with drifts of sand and grit. Pheasants raised bright heads from stony distances or dashes suddenly across the road. A rabbit darted under one wheel and was crushed. Far above, the harrier circled, waiting for the phaeton to roll away, and then plunged.

They gathered speed down a gentle slope and began to bowl along beside a palisade of cedars. Seed cones like plump little lanterns shook in the faint breeze of their passing. The road turned in through the green stockade and widened into a long straight drive. An avenue of limes masked all save a red brick gateway until they were nearly upon it, when the whole long frontage opened up with a flourish of turrets and ornamental cornices. Deborah gasped. Isabel flashed a quick pleased smile at her reaction. The body of the house was of grey stone save for the brick entrance. Flanking wings of mellow red brick were chequered with ornamental insets of chocolate-brown carstone.

'Lots of people have stuck bits and pieces on,' Isabel observed. 'Mother says it's a patchwork quilt rather than a house. The porch and the north end were done by some Tudor Stannard, and the south end by his son. The stones are from the old priory.' She waved vaguely to her left, but Deborah saw only a thick clump of oaks. Here, at least, someone had fought the infertile breck and conquered.

They wheeled under a row of white-morticed windows and turned again at the end of the house. Above were more recent, skittish additions: a pinnacled lantern topping the gable, and pepperpot turrets in each corner.

'That was my father's contribution. Justin used to play knights and varlets with me, and imprisoned maidens, and things like that.' Isabel peered up from beneath the carriage canopy. 'He scared me sometimes; he made it so convincing. Justin always throws himself heart and soul into whatever he's doing.'

They emerged beside a terrace facing south. Rock plants wove in and out of the stonework. A woman in plum-coloured brocade, with a glint of silver embroidery at her wrists, came out on the steps. Deborah admitted to herself that she had half-expected Justin Stannard to be waiting to greet her.

'So you have persuaded Miss Ritchie to visit us. I'm so glad. Welcome to Stannard Priory, my dear.'

Lady Stannard could be little more than fifty, but her face was that of an older woman. Her movements as Isabel introduced them were stiff: she kept her elbows close to her side and bunched her whole body strangely in on itself. But her greeting was expansive enough. She clasped Deborah's hand, and smiled unaffectedly.

'I'm so glad,' she repeated. Her eyes were dusky violet, and there was a faint mauve tinge in the skin below them. 'Yes.' She looked Deborah up and down approvingly. Taking Deborah's arm, she led her to the end of the terrace, with a view between clumps of oak and elm towards a glitter of distant water.

Isabel voiced Deborah's thoughts. 'Is Justin indoors?'

'He had to ride over to Meddleheath,' said her mother. 'It came to him on the spur of the moment. You know how these things come upon him.'

'Yes,' said Isabel. 'I do know.'

'He assured me he'd make the best possible speed and be home for luncheon, and that Miss Ritchie would then be given a full explanation for his not being here to greet her.'

There was a nonplussed silence. The three of them all depended, thought Deborah with some asperity, on the whims of one young man.

Lady Stannard waved at the slopes below the terrace. 'Well, now we have time for a little stroll before lunch. You must see my sunken garden, though it's not at its best this month. Let's walk down towards the priory first.'

A stream meandering along the foot of

the slope fed a number of small conduits. Sunk into the ground at intervals, masked by shrubs, were large rain butts.

'My husband had plans to extend grass and crops beyond the estate itself,' explained Lady Stannard. 'He dug marl-pits to provide new topsoil, but the sand keeps blowing, and the rabbits get at everything. And people here are so set in their ways, they won't turn their hands to a different way of life. Sooner scratch a living from skinning rabbits or knapping gunflints than from the land. Of course, shortage of water has always been such a problem, but if they had been prepared to farm as hard as my husband did . . . '

Deborah remembered the stream in the grounds of Saxwold Hall. Obviously houses and hamlets in this barren patch of England could have been established only where freshening brooks broke the dry surface.

Lady Stannard was holding forth on a subject she had loyally learnt parrot-fashion from her late husband. The streams and meres, she explained, had a way of drying up with little warning, as if sucked away from beneath. It was something to do with subterranean water levels, though the locals ascribed it, as you might expect, to witchcraft and the malice of resident spirits. The logical explanation . . .

Logical explanations? The thought of Saxwold Hall reminded Deborah of Beatrice's brooch. She was only half listening to Lady Stannard. There had to be some simple explanation for the appearance of that brooch, and of all the other mysteries.

As their feet padded down the grass, Lady Stannard said sharply: 'Haven't you found that so, Miss Ritchie?'

'I'm so sorry,' said Deborah. 'My attention was distracted by . . . a memory,' she said lamely.

'Oh, I do understand. You must have had so many things on your mind. I was saying that travelling as you have done, you must have found it difficult to establish close friendships.'

'My father had good friends in Midlothian. I've always been able to call on them when needed.'

'But you have rarely felt the need?' said Lady Stannard keenly. 'In any case, I was thinking of people of your own age.'

'I've had little opportunity, no.' Deborah thought of the elderly invalids of the spa towns, where the few people of her own age tended to be girls like herself: daughters chained to ailing fathers, or paid nurses and companions who, on the death of one patient, must seek another.

'You'll find no shortage of young admirers now.'

'So Mr. MacKenzie warned me.'

'Mr. MacKenzie?'

'Our family solicitor. Though I think of him more as an honorary uncle, as he's always been so close to us.'

'He takes his niece's welfare much to heart, from the sound of it. Very wise advice.'

Deborah had been taking in the landscape as vaguely as she had taken in Lady Stannard's disquisition on streams and meres. Now her attention was caught by a new feature in the scene. Clear of the trees, set on what appeared to be a moated island, was a grey stone ruin, its outline shrouded in a tangle of under-growth.

'That's the original priory.' Lady Stannard was glad to have another topic to fill in the time. 'It wasn't destroyed, as so many were, at the Dissolution of the Monasteries.'

'It looks fairly thoroughly destroyed to me,' Deborah observed.

'I'm afraid that's the work of the second baron. The first Lord Stannard in Henry's time was influential enough to buy the priory back from the Crown in order to complete the family chantry. It was never a large foundation, just a limb of the Cluniac priory at Castle Acre, used largely as a retreat for more ascetic members of the order.'

They must have been ascetic and self-denying in the extreme, thought Deborah, to have chosen to live there.

'The second baron wasn't much interested in the chantry or in much else on the spiritual plane,' Lady Stannard went on. 'He took a lot of the stones away for building the house. What was left has become dangerous. Nobody is allowed across the moat nowadays.'

Above the ruins rose the jagged remnant of an arch that might once have enclosed a chapel window. Supports had crumbled or been taken away until there was only this hooked claw, poised to tear down into its victim.

Deborah said: 'I suppose they're haunted? All the best ruins are.'

'Oh, without question. There are ghostly lights, and midnight revels, and hideous noises. So the local stories have it. We don't discourage them: it keeps poachers and other undesirable folk away.' She took a small gold watch from her waistband. 'Perhaps we should turn back.'

They made their way up the gentle slope, dominated by the grey and red mansion. From this angle, Deborah noticed that several upper windows were boarded up, and that the corner of a stable block badly needed repointing.

She said: 'Your son, the present Lord Stannard — he is carrying on his father's interest in land reclamation?'

'No, I fear not. Our older boy would

have done so. It was close to his heart. He was killed in a hunting accident. I think it was that which killed his father also.'

'I'm sorry. I had no idea.'

'No reason why you should have done, Miss Ritchie. In any event, Justin shows little interest. He had no real expectation of inheriting, and perhaps my husband didn't do enough to interest him in the affairs of the estate. Of course he has so many things to contend with.' Lady Stannard hastened to forestall any criticism. 'There are the problems of the magistracy, and the board of guardians and his work for the county militia. And he's an expert on the game laws.'

They climbed the steps to the terrace.

'I'm sure,' said Lady Stannard firmly, 'that when Justin has settled down, he'll accept the full responsibilities of his inheritance. The right wife will set him on the right path.'

Indoors, they crossed a small reception room and came into a soaring staircase hall that took Deborah's breath away. Its ceiling, a stucco imitation of fan vaulting, was a full three storeys up, the stairs descending in six sharply angled stages.

Justin was on the second landing. When he saw his mother and Deborah, he quickened his pace, skimming his right hand lightly down the baluster rail and then holding it out demandingly to Deborah as he reached the bottom step and strode across the hall. His hair was ruffled and he had the glow of the outdoors about him. Yet since returning, he had managed to take care over his appearance. His pearl-buttoned velvety brown cutaway coat sat perfectly, without a crease, across his slim shoulders.

'I have done my best to keep Miss Ritchie entertained in your absence,' said his mother petulantly. 'We didn't get to the gardens, but — '

'Mother is always so busy with her gardens.' Justin relinquished Deborah's hand unwillingly, maintaining his intense gaze. 'And, with her almshouses and her orphanage and the cottagers' clothing club and — '

'And keeping an eye on your household, so that there shall be no waste. You would never notice such things yourself.'

'How true.' Justin's eyes twinkled at Deborah.

Isabel, hearing their voices, came into the hall. 'Deborah.' She spoke the name firmly. 'If you would like to come to my room for a few minutes, I'll send my maid in, and then we shall all be ready for lunch.'

The maid brought a jug of hot water, and took the opportunity of appraising Deborah with saucy eyes. It was hard to think of this buxom little thing attending on the thoroughbred Isabel. When Deborah spoke to her, she emitted a surprisingly deep, throaty little chuckle, and bobbed away.

As they went down to lunch, Isabel confirmed Deborah's judgment. 'Miriam is becoming a sight too impertinent. I'm considering replacing her. But it's so tiresome trying to find a suitable girl from the villages, and no one from outside cares to come into service in the breckland.'

When they were seated at table, Justin Stannard said: 'Isabel already finds it natural to call you Deborah. Have we your permission to become Deborah, and Isabel, and Justin?'

Lady Stannard's stiff little hand made an involuntary movement. *Patience*, it said. And when Deborah mutely sought her counsel, the hand waved stiffly and fell to her lap again.

Justin said: 'Deborah, my purpose in riding to Meddleheath this morning was to urge all reasonable speed on old Abbott. You'll be pleased to know that there'll be the briefest of formal inquests, that nobody will contest its findings. If it suits you, the worthy Ormesby can conduct the funeral service the day after tomorrow.'

'But yesterday,' said Deborah, taken aback, 'I understood you didn't wish the procedure to be rushed through.'

He said: 'I confess my first reaction was to advise delay. In Gaunt's company, I find myself instinctively taking the opposite view from any which he may express.'

Deborah gave a rueful smile of complicity.

'I have changed my mind,' he went on, 'for Miss Ritchie's . . . for Deborah's sake. Her reasons for wanting to dispose of this unpleasant business are sound. Gaunt's would seem singularly suspicious were it not that, having been in London at the time of the fire, he could hardly have had any hand in it.'

'Justin!' protested his sister.

Deborah stared. 'Why should Sir Randall have had any hand in it, in any case?'

'The obscurity of Gaunt's motives and of his general conduct has always been a matter of concern to many of us.'

Lady Stannard drew herself up. 'I would prefer to drop this subject. At once.'

Justin went on remorselessly: 'I don't like the idea of Miss Ritchie staying at Saxwold Hall, even in his absence. Who's to say when he'll come back without warning? Or what strangeness he may be capable of? That place has too many dubious associations.'

'You were willing enough once,' said Isabel with downcast eyes, 'to entrust your sister to — '

'We've learned too much since. We

know he hastened his wife's death in his eagerness to advance his own career.'

'We know no such thing.' It was torn from Isabel.

'You see, Deborah, the mesmeric effect Gaunt can have on susceptible young ladies? I'm frightened for anyone who comes too closely under his influence.'

With tremulous dignity, Lady Stannard said: 'It's my belief that Sir Randall suffers in ways we don't understand, or should wish to. We know nothing of the truth. I grant you he has surrendered too completely to bitterness — '

'His conscience,' said Justin.

'We cannot judge. Whatever he did, or failed to do, he has spent years paying for it.'

'And has not paid nearly enough.' Justin's fingers tightened around the stem of his glass of hock. He turned to Deborah. 'Mother is right. I admit I can't stand the fellow, and have many sound reasons; as Isabel also must have, if she is honest. But they are no justification for involving you in the sordid tittle-tattle of the knappers' yard. Our purpose in inviting you here was to take your mind off sadness.'

Deborah was tempted to tell him about the brooch. But that would surely have provoked another tirade against Sir Randall Gaunt, solving nothing. Instead, she said: 'It's kind of you, Lord Stannard.'

'Justin.'

'Justin,' she said. 'I appreciate your kindness. But ... there *are* some questions still to be answered.'

'If there's any way in which I can set your mind at rest ... '

'That old woman,' said Deborah. 'The one who was talking to me when you came into the churchyard. Mrs. Pigle.'

'Some say she's our local witch,' he said lightly.

'She was the one who worked for Beatrice and Edwin when the other servants had gone.'

Justin was suddenly attentive. 'And what did she have to say?'

'She asked how we could be sure Beatrice died in the fire. Because she claimed Beatrice hadn't been there the week before it happened.'

'Where was she, then?'

'Mrs. Pigle didn't know. All she said was that up to a couple of days before the fire, when she left, Beatrice hadn't been at home.'

'Where could she have been?' asked Isabel.

Justin leaned across the table. 'Baseless rumours, mischief-making. That creature should never have been employed by the Flemings. It shows, I'm afraid, to what a state they had sunk. But to believe any word that any member of the Pigle family says . . . A more degenerate, inbred family it would be hard to find.'

'But where *was* Beatrice?' Deborah persevered.

Justin smote his forehead. 'Wherever she may have been, she was certainly home at Toft Warren the day before the fire. I saw her — I remember now. The old woman must have left by that time, if her story is to be believed. I distinctly remember passing Mrs. Fleming out riding, on her way home as I was cutting across Pedlar's Clump.'

'On her way home? From where?'

'We only exchanged the usual civilities. I had no reason to interrogate her.'

'She was her usual self?'

'I saw nothing amiss.'

'So she was there,' said Deborah. 'On the night of the fire she was at home.'

'It would be false to swear otherwise,' said Justin gently.

Lady Stannard sighed. 'And this is how we cheer Miss Ritchie up!'

Justin looked at Deborah. 'Do you still wish for a lengthy investigation?'

'No.'

'Then the coroner's certificate shall be issued.'

His mother tinkled a bell at her left hand. When fruit had been set on the table, she clasped her hands together and said: 'Justin was right. It really is not suitable that you should stay at Saxwold Hall. Disregarding his prejudices, you really would be more comfortable here.'

'Everything would be so much easier,' Isabel added her plea. 'You can have the services of Miriam. We will drive you to the funeral, we can take you to your train — '

'Not so fast,' said Justin. 'I'd like to think Deborah would spend a few more days with us. We can offer her a place in which to recover, to consider what she wishes to do.'

They were remarkably similar to Randall Gaunt's words. Everybody wanted her to make up her mind about something: Gaunt implying that she should decide to leave and not come back, Justin Stannard that she should linger.

But some infernal stubbornness within her made her say the opposite of what she wished to say. 'I think I owe it to Sir Randall to pass the remaining time at Saxwold Hall. He would be offended if, in his absence, I moved away.' Especially if she moved to the home of someone with whom he was on such bad terms.

'Let him be offended, then,' growled Justin.

'Your scruples do you credit, my dear,' Lady Stannard said stiffly. 'If you wish to honour his hospitality, it would be wrong of us to influence you in any way.'

Deborah didn't want to turn away from

Justin, or from this house and family that had already made her feel welcome and that she belonged . . . or might conceivably belong. Yet she knew she had to go back to Saxwold Hall. The brooch had told her nothing, but there might be something else there that would at last speak clearly.

'You must let us send a carriage to take you to the funeral service,' Lady Stannard was saying. 'It can be sent to bring you here afterwards. Or to take you to Ingmere station when it suits you.' She looked at her son. 'I think there can be no doubt about such an arrangement?'

'None, Mother.'

But when he and Isabel were accompanying Deborah back across the breck, Justin asked: 'It is simply a matter of politeness that takes you back to Saxwold Hall?'

'What else should it be?'

'That is what troubles me. I can't imagine what solace you will find there.'

Nor could Deborah.

6

The funeral of the pitifully few charred bones took place on a still, bright morning. Justin and Isabel collected Deborah and took her to the service, knelt beside her in the church, and stood beside her as the single unnecessarily large coffin was lowered into its hole in the earth. When she could no longer hold back her tears, each of them put a hand below her elbows. It was more than a physical support; they made her feel that this was a family affair and that she was no longer alone.

Edwin's father had arrived for the ceremony. His uncanny resemblance to Deborah's own father almost undid her composure. Like the late Colonel Ritchie, General Peveril Fleming limped from the pain of old wounds; and, like Colonel Ritchie towards the end, had a tendency to wander in his mind and speech. He fought the tendency with a military, snappish impatience: a martinet, forcing himself to stand erect at the graveside. He was a soldier, used to sudden death and quick burials. Only one suppressed little whimper revealed his innermost feelings as the first handful of earth thudded onto the coffin lid.

Afterwards, the living had nothing to do but drift away and get on with living. The rector shook hands solemnly with Deborah, and then with Justin and Isabel. He did the same with General Fleming, and instinctively spoke in a louder tone than he had used with Deborah. The general responded with a 'Hm . . . yes . . . thought you made a good job of it, Reverend. I'm obliged to you.'

'You will lunch with us, sir?' Justin set the pattern, drawing them all together again. General Fleming looked momentarily resentful of the young man's easy assumption of authority; but then, leaning on his stick and holding himself in against a stab of pain, he was glad to accept. The Reverend Gerald Ormesby was delighted to join them.

When they reached Stannard Priory, it

was evident their attendance had been taken for granted. A cold buffet had been spread upon a long sideboard table in a sunlit room that opened onto the terrace. Lady Stannard was waiting for them, and in spite of the nature of the occasion enjoyed playing hostess.

Justin offered Deborah cold meats, served her himself instead of summoning the footman, and poured her a glass of wine.

His mother swept up. 'Justin, you are not to monopolise Miss Ritchie.'

'But that's precisely my intention, Mother.'

'I am sure she will wish to exchange some remarks with General Fleming.'

Deborah dreaded the awkward minutes when they must share condolences, and she would see again, as she had seen in church, the pathetic resemblances to her father.

In fact, the general was making a determined, deliberate recovery from the melancholy of the morning. 'Wretched business.' It was dismissive and unsentimental.

The footman carried his plate and glass out to the wide stone balustrade of the terrace. General Fleming held his glass up to Deborah, drank, and said:

'Sorry I never met your father, my'dear. Heard fine reports of him.'

'They were all true,' said Deborah.

'Odd.' He blinked at her. 'You're so like Beatrice, yet not the least bit like her. Eh?' He set the glass down carefully. 'Rotten for you, this mess. You never met my boy?'

Deborah shook her head. 'The wedding came at an awkward time, when — '

'Rushed. Edwin all over.'

'And Beatrice.'

'My boy was the one.' He winced. 'It was up to him.' He had suffered a mortal blow, but sought to soothe Deborah, shouldering his son rather than Beatrice with whatever blame there might be. 'He made a fool of himself in London, and then again in Bath. I'd hoped when he got here, the different way of life . . . healthy exercise, some decent shooting . . . ' He crouched against another wrench of pain. 'But it must have got even worse. Thank God there's an end to it.'

'It was all a terrible accident,' said Deborah.

'An accident?'

'You think there was something else? You think,' asked Deborah uncertainly, 'there ought to be more searching enquiries?'

'Certainly not.' His stick rang on a flagstone. 'Something terrible has happened, yes. But it's over, they're buried in consecrated ground. Who's to say, if we found out too much of what was behind it, that they might prove . . . ' He would not let himself finish.

Lady Stannard brought the rector out on to the terrace. As they approached, Deborah said: 'I've suggested to Mr. Ormesby that I provide a memorial inside the church, in keeping with the restoration he plans.'

'We shall do it together,' said the general. His eyes brightened at the notion. 'Now, sir.' He waved the rector closer. 'Miss Ritchie and I have decided to present a fitting memorial for my son and daughter-in-law.'

Ormesby beamed. 'Miss Ritchie did say she was contemplating — '

'From where I was sitting this morning, I noticed one singular lack. You have no suitable lectern.'

'The remains of the old one are piled up in a pew,' said Ormesby regretfully.

'Miss Ritchie?'

'Certainly,' said Deborah. 'It's a splendid idea! A new lectern, worthily carved — with a stone plinth this time, to provide a less vulnerable foundation.'

'Then it's settled.'

General Fleming looked pleased. The rector smiled at him, and at Deborah, and at Lady Stannard.

'There is a dependable stonemason in Ingmere,' said the rector, eager to have the details settled while his benefactors were still on the scene, 'and I've heard well of a carpenter some miles away, on the other side of Lantern Mere.'

'Lantern Mere?' Deborah echoed.

Lady Stannard laughed. 'Another local superstition. It takes its name from the marsh lights that dance over it at night.

The cottagers believe them to be carried by the 'lantern men'. You'll get used to all these hauntings.'

'I shall hardly have time to get used to them,' said Deborah, 'since I must soon be on my way home.'

Justin came out on to the terrace and stood transfixed by her words. When it was time to leave, he said that he would travel in the carriage taking her back to Saxwold Hall, and General Fleming to the inn by Ingmere railway station. The general was set down first. As they shook hands, he gave her a smile that touched her heart — a dashing young man's smile that he would have given a beautiful young girl when he was fifty years younger. Deborah wished that she too could leave the carriage now, walk up the station approach, and be borne away on a train.

On the last stretch of the journey, Justin broke a long silence. 'I overheard you telling my mother that you intended to leave for home.'

'Tomorrow,' she said. 'There is a lot to be done, a lot to decide.'

'You would find it easier to make the right decisions if you stayed with us for a while. The priory had a good reputation, once, as a retreat for those who wished to meditate on their present and future problems.'

'I fancy I shall find it easier,' she whispered, 'in more familiar surroundings.'

He leaned across the swaying carriage. 'I will not let you go, Deborah.'

'Lord Stannard, please . . . '

'Justin,' he said. 'We have agreed that my name is Justin and yours Deborah.'

'Lord Stannard.'

He drew slowly back and quirked his lips to show that he took her rejection in good part; but she could sense his frustration.

As the carriage turned onto the drive, he turned once more before the entrance to Saxwold Hall and said, 'Isabel and I will take you to the train in the morning. There is a connection for the northbound line at nine o'clock.'

'Sir Randall left instructions that I might call upon his coachman at any time. I would not wish you to come so far.'

'Would you not?' He looked her full in the eyes, his gaze as fierce as any she had ever seen in a man. 'You would go to the station alone, rather than with your friends?'

'I did not mean — '

'Isabel and I will accompany you to the station,' he said, 'if it's truly your wish to go.'

'That is what I wish.'

She was lying. And because it was untrue, and because in his presence she was afraid of the truth, she said it all the more forcibly.

* * *

On her last night in Saxwold Hall, the house had still told her nothing. Many times she had taken out Beatrice's brooch, staring at it as some fortune-teller might, hoping for some mystic revelation.

In those empty two days before the funeral, she had walked in the garden and apparently aimlessly through the house.

105

Mrs. Thurton or a footman would appear at intervals out of nowhere, opening doors or politely steering her to a comfortable library, or into a little sitting-room that would have been more agreeable had there been any sensation of its having been used during the last few years. How many years had Randall Gaunt said? Nine since his wife's death: nine years and a little over five weeks now. And more than a year since Beatrice last set foot here.

Deborah listened vainly for tell-tale resonances. The hours of late afternoon and early evening dragged interminably. As she was in her room preparing for the early dinner agreed on with Mrs. Thurton, she heard a sudden quickening of footsteps up and down stairs, and the faint rumble of wheels slowing into the stableyard. A draught sighed along the corridor and under her door. Again there was a hush; yet she had the impression of some muffled shock continuing to vibrate through the very air of the place.

As she went down to the hall, the study door opened and Boynton came out, crossing the hall without noticing her. He carried a tray with a crystal tumbler and a full decanter on it, hurrying towards the corridor that led to the back of the house.

Deborah went into the dining-room. She had been there for five minutes when Mrs. Thurton looked in, said breathlessly, 'Oh, there you are, miss,' and disappeared. Soon she returned with a timorous little maid bearing a tureen. 'Alice will look after you, miss.'

Deborah ate alone and in silence. At intervals, Alice fussed in and out. Just once towards the end of the meal, Mrs. Thurton looked in to ask if everything was satisfactory. It was foolish to suppose she was glancing in merely to make sure that Deborah was still safely at table.

Deborah felt a need to go out and savour the warm evening air, to catch the last touch of the sun on her brow. She stood up and left the room, half-expecting to find a sentry at the door, but there was none.

She strolled in a lost, lonely world. From the bank of the stream, she looked up at the top floor of Saxwold Hall.

Within the battlemented parapet was the gleam of a sloping glass roof. She made a leisurely circuit of the house, her gaze answered by only blank, unseeing windows. The water tower darkened in silhouette against orange streaks of cloud.

Without warning, a rumble shook the ground. The shudder was that of the steam pump starting up. The brick outbuilding of the boiler house emitted puffs of smoke from its chimney. Beside it, close to a side door leading into the wing, was another squat brick building with a cast-iron door in one side. Drawing closer, she saw the blackened edges of brick around the door and framing a grille across the top. It was a large incinerator, sheltered from the wind. But there was no path to it along which garden rubbish might be carted; and when she peered down through the grille, there was no smell of burnt weeds and cuttings. It was a different smell, like burnt hair or hide. Or bones.

Deborah turned away. The latch of the door was close to her hand. Getting her bearings, she looked up and thought she could identify the window of her room — the window from which she had watched a girl run towards what must have been this very door.

She tried the latch and found the door open. Beside it was a heavily barred window. In the dark corridor within, she caught a glimpse of a narrow staircase with the outline of another door at its foot. This probably led to a gunroom into which the man of the house could stump direct from outdoors.

Slowly, as she ventured in, the outer door swung shut behind her, plunging her into pitch blackness. She groped out in search of the wall. Her hand slid along a line of beading and reached the frame of the other door. A little way down was a knob. It turned under her fingers, and when she pushed the door open there came a welcome glimmer of light through the barred window, sufficient to orient herself. Faintly she could make out a case of guns on the far wall. Taking a step into the room, she saw more glass cases. Curious, she bent nearer the one by her right hip.

It was one of a sequence of small glass-fronted display cabinets in which were exposed shrivelled, contorted, splayed and gnarled shapes Deborah found unrecognisable. Then the nearest began to take on hideous familiarity. It was the torso of a dog, its rib cage opened out and the skin pickled to a deep tan. As her eyes grew accustomed to the twilight, she saw that the other exhibits were slices, limbs, bony segments of animals preserved and staked down in a charnel parade.

Trying to prop the door open so there should be some illumination as she backed out, she stumbled and fell towards the banister rail of the steep stairs. The door slammed shut, and she was clawing out into darkness once more. The rail creaked as she steadied herself. She put one foot forward and found the lowest tread of the stairs. It creaked even more loudly than the rail had done.

Somewhere far above, a door was flung open. 'Who's there?' It was the voice of Sir Randall Gaunt.

Deborah floundered in a sightless panic, trying to steer herself round to face the outer door. But when she took a step she jarred against the door jamb of that hideous room again. Light spilled down the stairs.

'How did you know I was back? How *do* you get to know? It won't do, not tonight. You'll have to go away. I'm in no mood for . . . '

Deborah turned to face up the steep flight into the radiance of a candle lamp. Behind it, Gaunt's shape loomed cloudy and predatory, leaning out in preparation for a swoop.

'Well,' he said. Well. Miss Ritchie.'

'The door,' said Deborah hoarsely. 'The side door there, it closed behind me. I couldn't see. I had no idea where I was.'

He came slowly down a few more steps. 'I suppose you thought to find a short cut through the house from this wing.' He was offering her an excuse, but his voice was heavy with irony. 'I apologise for the complexities of our domestic maze.'

'I'm sorry. I didn't know you had returned. I shouldn't have come this way.'

'No call to apologise, Miss Ritchie. I

invited you to use Saxwold Hall for as long as it suited you. You were free to explore any corner that took your fancy.'

'Sir Randall, if you would be kind enough to direct the light so that I may find my way out — '

'No, Miss Ritchie.' The raw edge of his tone flailed her ears. 'Since you are here, you may as well come and inspect the witch doctor's den. They'll have told you, or they'll soon make haste to tell you, what sinister practices are performed under my roof. I invite you to see for yourself.'

He began to return upstairs. Deborah began apprehensively to follow him. Justin had spoken of the man's mesmeric power.

At the top of the third flight a door stood open, and inside the shadows of dusk fled away from the candle lamp. Gaunt stood by the door until she had passed him, then closed it and set the lamp on a table. Four more candles flickered in brackets at the far end of the glass-roofed laboratory. There was a surgical couch, and on a long table lay an armoury of scalpels and instruments whose use she did not care to guess at. Along one wall were shelves crowded with glass jars of specimens as warped and disturbing as those she had seen in the room far below.

'They say I'm a witch doctor!' Gaunt extended one hand towards a bowl of dried herbs and suddenly knocked it flying. An acrid, musky scent filled the room. 'Well, see for yourself.' He paced up and down. 'See where they come — those who aren't afraid to come. The ones who *are* afraid mutter their own spells to themselves. And I'd not be surprised to learn they stick pins in wax images of me. And those who are afraid but still have to come to me, desperate enough to seek me out and come fawning . . . ' He planted himself before her. 'Which are you, Miss Ritchie?'

'I'm neither afraid nor fawning.'

But she was afraid of what he could possibly mean and of the tautness in the vein down his neck and of his strained, straining eyes — the eyes of a man near breaking point.

Had he been drinking? But close beside her was the tray Boynton had been carrying, and on it the glass was still clean, the decanter untouched. On an accompanying tray, food congealed on a plate.

Gaunt sagged against the couch. 'I must apologise, Miss Ritchie. You took me unawares.'

'I must leave you to . . . to your work.'

She looked for a way out other than that narrow, dark flight up which she had been reluctantly drawn.

'You are not your sister,' he fired suddenly at her. 'She was only a sketch for the real thing.'

There was a deferential tap against a panel in the far wall. When Gaunt called 'Come in', a door opened and Mrs. Thurton stood there.

'I'm sorry, sir, I didn't realise — '

'Come in, Mrs. Thurton.'

The housekeeper eyed Deborah with disapproval, then transferred this to the plate on the tray. 'You haven't eaten a thing, sir.'

'No. I'm afraid I forgot it was there.'

'I'll bring you something else.'

'No,' said Gaunt wearily. 'No, I have little appetite.' As Mrs. Thurton removed the tray, he added: 'Perhaps you'll show Miss Ritchie back to her room. She lost her way in our labyrinth.'

'Yes, sir,' said Mrs. Thurton sceptically.

★　★　★

Justin and Isabel arrived in good time to drive Deborah to the station. Mrs. Thurton viewed her departure with undisguised relief, but could not resist a carping thrust.

'The master gave instructions that you should use his carriage if you need it.'

'Lord Stannard and his sister were most anxious to accompany me to the station,' said Deborah. 'I would hate to hurt their feelings.'

And since there was no sign of her host even coming to wish her a comfortable journey, she was doubly glad of this freely given, affectionate company.

As they drove away, she saw Mrs. Thurton plodding up to the attic to report to Sir Randall that he had the place to himself again. Perhaps she would find that he had at last turned to the decanter and was still sleeping off its effects.

'We ought not to have let you go,' said Isabel.

'But Deborah told us she felt under an obligation. The obligation of the fly,' said Justin mockingly, 'when caught in the spider's web. Fortunately the spider did not come back in time to devour its prey.'

She could not tell them that Gaunt had in fact come back, or how he had spoken. Whatever ill feeling might lie between these two men, whatever tangled lives they lived here, were none of her concern. Soon she would be gone.

As the train clanked in beside the station platform, Isabel made a last plea. 'We can't persuade you to change your mind and stay a while?'

Deborah shook her head, not trusting herself to speak.

Justin stood erect, silent and unsmiling. At last he held out his hand, and while the porter took her trunk to the luggage

116

van they stared for a long moment at each other.

'Goodbye,' she said.

'I think not,' said Justin. 'Oh, I shall ensure that it's not so.'

She was on her way. The scrubland rolled away behind, the green plains spread out beside the line and then in their turn fell away, and the landscape shifted and changed. Church steeples and a great cathedral marked off the miles, and there came the hour she could scarcely believe was real when, in the yellow pool under a gas lamp, the cab set her down in Charlotte Street.

The door was opened by Mrs. Muir, who looked both pleased and startled. 'We weren't expecting you back so soon, Miss Deborah.'

Fresh from a world preoccupied with Beatrice's death, Deborah quickly adjusted to one in which the news had not yet been announced. She waited until the housekeeper had bustled her into what had been her mother's sitting-room and now was her own, and sat down and summarised the facts in as level and dispassionate a tone as she could muster.

Mrs. Muir let out a sob, clasped her hands together, said 'No' and waved towards the mantelpiece, and then said 'No' again and began to cry. Deborah, reeling with fatigue, got up again and put her arm round her.

'Sit down, Mrs. Muir. It takes some getting used to, I know.'

'But there's that letter.' Mrs. Muir pointed again towards the mantelpiece. 'Coming as it did, just after you'd gone, I didnae think there was much sense in sending it on. She'd be saying whatever it was she had to say to you herself.'

Deborah took the envelope from the letter rack. She recognised the handwriting, just as Mrs. Muir had done.

It was a letter from Beatrice.

7

A letter from the dead? Or from someone who, Mrs. Pigle had intimated, might not even have been in the house when it burned down?

When Mrs. Muir had tearfully withdrawn, Deborah opened the envelope. The letter was dated the day before the fire. In the top right-hand corner, Beatrice had scribbled the name of Toft Warren House. So Mrs. Pigle was wrong: Beatrice had been there at the end.

The scrawl was authentically Beatrice's. The whole tone of the letter was as loudly and characteristically Beatrice as if she had been crying out in the room — crying out confusedly and from the page, spattered with underlining and ink smudges.

She wrote that Deborah must not, after all, come to stay at Toft Warren. Too many dreadful things had taken place. She could not offer hospitality worthy of the

119

name, couldn't let her into the house, hoped she was in time to stop her setting out. But they must meet, she had to talk to Deborah, she *had* to talk.

Even when I tell you, you'll hardly credit the shame of it, but I must talk to *somebody*, and who *else*? You have to help me, please, Deborah. It cannot be here close to where it happened and to *him* who brought it upon me, but somewhere far away. There's no safety here, I dare not stay. What I have done and what has been done to me must all be told, but not here where *he* is still able to reach out for me — and it may be worse than last time. I am newly come out of a week in hell, and my body and my mind are tortured with shame of temptation, and I *must* come to you. Write, *please*, write to invite me to stay with you. Only do not say one word about what I have written to you, or Edwin may forbid it, for he is beside himself on account of this other demon of a man and the shame of it; though it is *his own damnable doing*, and I do not know how we shall live now or who I can turn to. Please write to say that you cannot come here, but that you wish me to visit you and console you and *soon, please*. Deborah.

Deborah went to see Lewis MacKenzie in his chambers behind the Tolbooth. She broke the news of Beatrice's death. Mr. MacKenzie lifted rheumy eyes towards the ceiling, as yellow with pipe smoke as his nostrils were with snuff, and mumbled what might have been an ancient curse or benediction. She showed him Beatrice's letter.

He creased it between his fingers, muttered, and said: 'Aye, it looks like a gey fine mix-up she got herself into. And no more than I'd have expected, poor silly lass.'

'What shall we do?'

'Do? Are we no a wee bit late to be doing anything now?'

He made her sit facing him and go over the story in detail. Hearing her own voice quicken at mention of Justin Stannard and noticing Mr. MacKenzie's bushy right eyebrow twitch quizzically, she dodged away from that subject and tried to keep the narrative matter-of-fact.

When she had finished, he creaked back in his chair and pushed Beatrice's letter back across the desk. 'Since yon young woman's dead and past our helping, I'd be thinking that's an end to it. It's no a happy memory and yon's no a letter ye'll be likely to forget in a hurry. But the fire has destroyed, and there's no sense in raking over the ashes. Now there's the legal procedures, and those you'll be leaving to me. The poor soul's money will come to you now, and I'll not be sorry to see it arranged that way.'

'But we can't just draw a line under Beatrice and say that's that . . . '

'That's just what you'd best be doing. It's too long you've had to fret over your father, and there's no use in fretting over your sister.' He raised his voice in one of his mock rages. 'Will ye no be getting out o' here into the fresh air and letting the past blow right out of your head?'

Mr. MacKenzie thumped the desk once and switched without more ado to a discussion of steps he had taken during her brief absence regarding the deeds of the house, transfer of her father's investments, and a number of financial matters to which she assented without troubling to listen too attentively. Afterwards, she took his advice and went out into the fresh air.

It was good to walk again up the steep cobbled streets and through the lanes and wynds in which she could never get lost, emerging onto sudden vistas of the castle and spires, the New Town below, and the observatory and monuments heaped up on Calton Hill. She paused to pat a horse snuffling contentedly over a drinking trough. The warm smell of the horse's body mingled with a sweet and bitter potpourri of other smells — tang of gutter and courtyard and a baker's shop and some strong, reeking tobacco; and something else, a dusty but purifying breeze that blew capriciously in from the hills. It was wonderful to know that beyond the end of a street there would be no flat waste of scrubland, no desert of sand and flint, but more groves of houses, towers, high tenements and bustling traffic.

Mr. MacKenzie and his wife invited her to dine at their home. Fellow guests were two old friends of the MacKenzies' and a young notary of about Deborah's age who was too shy to say much of consequence. The older couple asked whether she now proposed to settle in Edinburgh, and were sympathetically sure she had done enough travelling to last anyone a lifetime.

Deborah wrote a carefully phrased letter to Sir Randall Gaunt thanking him for the accommodation and facilities he had placed at her disposal. His flinty house was a million miles away, yet somehow she had not escaped. She was glad to be home, but there was something missing.

On the fourth day after her return, Justin and Isabel Stannard called upon her. They had accepted, Isabel explained, a long-standing invitation to stay with friends at Leith. While here they wished to see as much of Edinburgh as possible, and it had occurred to her that if Deborah could spare a few hours she would be an ideal guide.

Justin let his sister do the talking — had perhaps primed her for it — while his gaze roamed hungrily over Deborah's face. She was tempted to say how strange a coincidence it was that they had accepted what they called a longstanding invitation to this part of the world so soon after meeting her in theirs. But she suspected that Justin would turn the tables by airily admitting his motives, as he had done that day on the terrace with his frank declaration to his mother that he intended to monopolise Miss Ritchie.

She said: 'After the kindness you showed me last week, the least I can do — '

'No.' At last Justin spoke aloud. 'No, that will never do. There's no question of your owing us any return. Your company was more than adequate repayment. If you will escort *us* for a day or two, it must be only because you have the time and will be caused no inconvenience . . . and that you wish it.'

Put like that, it offered no alternative.

'Most assuredly I wish it,' Deborah said. And it was true.

These last few days, she had quietly enjoyed retracing her steps through byways of memory and long-familiar, reassuring streets. Now she enjoyed it twice as much. Princes Street took on new vitality, the military band in the gardens played with greater gusto, the Royal Mile acquired a diadem of new splendours when seen through other eyes. This was what gave such an added sparkle: seeing it all afresh because it was fresh to Justin and Isabel. Courtyards off the Lawnmarket, drab and dulled by long acquaintanceship, became romantic as she recounted their history. Justin bent towards her to hear the old tales of Mary and Holyrood and Bonnie Prince Charlie's heralds proclaiming his father king at the city cross.

When she pointed out the balcony from which Argyll had watched his enemy Montrose on the way to execution, his eyes gleamed as if he were, for a few moments, living the part of the rapacious Argyll. Isabel was the one who asked the most questions, but it was with Justin that Deborah most deeply shared her affections and insights, recalling and re-learning her city's history for his benefit. Gradually it became apparent that he was listening to the cadences of her voice rather than the information she was imparting, watching the movements of her lips for their own sake, his gaze sometimes lingering on a strand of her hair or on her throat.

She had been used to dining out occasionally on the Continent, but in her own country it was still a new and somewhat daring custom. Justin, however, took it for granted that she and Isabel would accompany him to a restaurant one evening — and in his choice showed a knowledge of fashionable Edinburgh which went beyond his pretence of being a naive stranger in need of guidance. Her décolletage was raked by the spur of his glance, and she prayed he would not discern the tightening response of her breasts.

'Your host is seeing little of you,' she challenged.

Justin shrugged. 'Angus understands well enough.'

'Which is more than I do.'

'I don't think that is true. I think, Deborah, you know which way my thoughts are tending. After the ordeals you have recently undergone, it is too soon to speak, that I appreciate, but — '

'Yes. Too soon to speak of anything.'

He bowed his head but she felt he was pleased with himself. It was no real rebuff, and they both knew it.

'Incidentally,' he said, deftly turning the conversation while she recovered herself, 'Angus tells me your grandfather was the Ritchie of Bengal. A great nabob, by all accounts.'

'He was a loyal company man. He died long before I was born.'

Colonel Ritchie had never talked at length about his father. Such details of her grandfather's career as had come Deborah's way were culled from other people's gossip and writings. She had read of one of two violent episodes and of a Parliamentary attack on the corrupt malpractices of the East India Company in general, and its powerful servant Colin Ritchie in particular. She fancied that her father, an upright soldier with no taste for politics or commerce, was half-ashamed of the sources of the family wealth. Deborah herself had been startled by her inheritance and by the awareness that responsibility for its use or misuse was hers from now on.

Justin must have listened as assiduously to his friend as he had done to Deborah, for he offhandedly revealed a considerable knowledge of the Ritchie family and its fortunes. He must have set himself to verify her status before deciding the level on which their acquaintanceship should be continued, if at all.

As they descended Arthur's Seat to stroll beside Duddingston Loch, he said lightly: 'I imagine Beatrice's own expectations were never of a high order?'

'She was comfortable.'

'Not a description I'd have chosen for her. Your mother must have been a remarkable woman, to produce two daughters so unalike.'

Like enough, thought Deborah, for Sir

Randall Gaunt to have been disturbed by the resemblance at first sight. With Beatrice in her mind, she thought too of that unfathomable letter. Impulsively she snapped open the tortoiseshell clip of her reticule and took out the folded sheet of paper. 'Perhaps there *ought* to have been more inquiries.'

Justin stood quite still to read it. It took him an age. He did not move a muscle, but his face paled.

'Whatever is it?' asked Isabel restively.

'I think you would be happier not seeing it.'

Isabel put out her hand, intent on discovering what disturbed him so. He seemed reluctant to let the paper go from between his fingers, but then passed it to her. He remained pale and tight-lipped.

Deborah said: 'She must have been on her way back from the post when you saw her.'

'Hm?' He roused himself. 'Oh, yes. You must be right. When she was riding home, yes.' He stared at the sheet of paper quivering like a leaf in his sister's hand. 'What can it mean?'

'It would be wrong of me to speculate. But Beatrice's footsteps, and her horse's footsteps, led her too often to a certain door.'

Isabel looked wretchedly up from the letter.

'What are you trying to say?' asked Deborah.

'I'm trying to say nothing.'

'You can't do a man an injustice on the strength of anything as unbalanced as this.' Isabel made to hand the letter back to Deborah, but her brother took it from her and began rereading it.

Deborah said: 'There's a name you're not speaking, either of you.'

'The name of a man,' murmured Justin, 'who was in great haste to have the formalities and the funeral over and done with.'

'I like to think that the haste was meant to spare my feelings — as it was with you.'

Sceptical silence was Justin's only answer.

Isabel said: 'Deborah, whatever destroyed Beatrice in the end may have been of her own making.' Her voice rose. 'There were times when she seemed all too willing to forget she was a married woman.'

'And times,' said Justin, 'when our friend seemed only too willing to help her forget.'

He refolded the letter and returned it to Deborah. As her reticule clicked shut on it, she said: 'What is this baleful influence that Sir Randall Gaunt exercises? What haven't you told me?'

'Gaunt,' said Justin, 'thinks of women as anatomical specimens for study and dissection, no more.'

Isabel moaned faintly.

'The mechanics of life are his obsession,' Justin stormed on, 'rather than life itself.'

Deborah recalled that haunted face she had seen that last late afternoon at Saxwold Hall. What had happened to the man in London — and what practices had he returned to? She said: 'Sir Randall's wife — '

'Was in a sickness from which she might have been saved by patient nursing

132

and proven medical methods. But that wasn't enough for Gaunt. As an anatomist, he wanted to see for himself, wanted his own wife used for experiment. He forced an operation upon her. And when she died in agony, instead of learning his lesson he pressed on even more eagerly. He sought new ... *material.* New corpses. If they were alive when they started, they finished as corpses.'

'Justin ... ' Isabel touched his arm. ' ... can't we leave the dead in peace?'

'What about the living who run the risk of an un-peaceful death, so long as he is allowed to continue?'

What about Beatrice? Deborah silently asked herself the question, trying to fit the words and phrases and underlining in the letter to Randall Gaunt's physical presence and manner.

Suddenly Justin said: 'This is no day for gloom. What's done cannot be undone — and there's no gain in brooding over it.'

The three of them remained subdued, thinking private thoughts for most of the day.

Next morning Justin and Isabel called again upon Deborah, by which time she had received another, very different letter. It came from Lady Stannard and entreated Miss Ritchie to accompany Justin and Isabel on their homeward journey. She had only seen the breckland in distressing circumstances. Autumn was coming, the countryside would soon be at its best, she would find the colours ravishing. Nothing could be simpler than for Justin and Isabel to bring her back to Stannard Priory for the holiday she needed. She would be in good hands. And it would please Lady Stannard so much.

Justin sparkled. 'What an admirable suggestion! She's right, Deborah. You must surely see that. You have not given Norfolk a fair trial.'

'I did not know I was under any obligation to do so.'

'No obligation. Merely the pleasure of it for all of us.'

'I am but newly home from your brecklands.'

'Deborah, we have been privileged to

see your splendid city through your eyes. Please let us return the favour. Come and see the brecks as we . . . as *I* see them.'

'Justin.' Instinctively she put her hand on his arm. Before she could draw it away, his right hand had closed on hers and his fingers were pressing down on hers. 'This letter is all part of a plot. You planted it in her mind before you left,' she accused him. 'It was all calculated before you even set out.'

'When a man knows his own mind, it would be foolish to leave anything to chance. He must back his convictions.'

'What is in your mind, then?'

'I will tell you when I am sure that it is in your mind also.'

The invitation was, as she had known it must be, his own. Gently his grip was tightening. He was wooing her at a measured pace, the pace and style of a stately dance, relying on their steps to bring them inevitably together. And when they had met, and the tempo quickened . . . ?

She made an excuse to take Justin and Isabel to meet Mr. MacKenzie. Perhaps his sardonic common sense would save her . . .

Justin was respectful in the attorney's presence, but wasted little time. Smoothly he contrived an alliance between them. Surely Mr. MacKenzie would agree that Miss Ritchie needed to be released from the past, with the help and understanding of true friends. A change of scene would fit her to deal more calmly with family memories and her future prospects when she returned.

'Ye have it in mind that she'll be returning?' interposed Mr. MacKenzie with a flash of his normal asperity.

Justin managed to make them all believe that the two poles of the civilised world were the heart of the breckland and the heart of Midlothian. He praised Edinburgh with a grace which made MacKenzie snort and glow, his usual reaction to any compliment offered to himself, his profession, or his city. Then, with the most skilful shift of emphasis, Justin was retaining the old man's interest as he conducted him towards Stannard Priory and the East Anglian heath. Justin withdrew, taking Isabel with him and leaving Mr. MacKenzie and Deborah together.

'Yon young cockerel knows what he wants.' MacKenzie took a liberal pinch of snuff. 'Aye, a gey fine young strutter, your young lordship.'

'Do you think it would be right for me to take such a trip back there, so soon?'

'Are ye telling me I have any say in the matter? I ken fine ye've already made up your mind, so what's all this but a waste of my time?'

'Then I ought to accept Lady Stannard's invitation?'

'Lady Stannard's invitation!' He snorted derisively. 'It sounds a good family, and ye ken by now how to look after yourself. Is that not so?' After a pause he added: 'One thing. Ye'd best be staying away from that other one, that Sir Randall who offered you his roof that first time.'

'What has Sir Randall to do with it?'

'There was talk in Nicolson Street this forenoon, at the college.' Nicolson Street meant inevitably, to everyone, the Royal

137

College of Surgeons of Edinburgh. 'I caught the name,' he said. 'It would seem the Royal College of Surgeons in London has severely censured the man. Found guilty of conducting dangerous and unethical anatomical experiments, and dabbling with drugs and neuro-hypnosis. His lectureship in anatomy has been suspended.'

Deborah realised that this must have been hanging over Gaunt when he hurried home to deal with the aftermath of the fire on his property, and then returned to London; and that when he returned distraught and shut himself away in his attic, it was because sentence had been passed. She thought of those exhibits preserved downstairs, and the glass jars and whatever else there might be, hidden away, at the top of the bleak grey house.

MacKenzie knew no further details. But the thought of anatomical experiments was one to send a shudder through any respectable household. In Edinburgh of all places it had gruesome associations: it was not so many years since Burke and

Hare ceased their grisly methods of supplying cadavers to the anatomist, Dr. Knox.

She said: 'I see no danger of our paths crossing again.'

'Ye could aye find yourself on the same roads again. There's a magnetism in it, sometimes . . . Ye'll not be going back simply to prowl about and fash yerself o'er Beatrice?'

Deborah wavered, then: 'No, that's not why I'm going.'

'So you're going. That's settled, anyway.'

She got up and leaned across his desk to kiss his brow.

'Aye.' He went purple. 'Aye, well.'

He insisted that this time she must surely not travel without a maid. The girl Mrs. MacKenzie had found for her, she was shaping well? Deborah agreed that Kirstie Hamilton was coming along very nicely, but she wondered if the girl would be happy leaving her native Scotland for a week or two at short notice. MacKenzie said that the girl was lucky to be in such good service and to be given the chance to travel, and then added: 'A week or two, is it? You'll not be expecting to stay on?'

'I have no such plans, no.'

'I'm thinking that maybe the plans'll be made for ye. He has a way wi' him.'

*   *   *

Kirstie Hamilton was competent but shy. When she met the footman who was to accompany them on the journey to Stannard Priory, she was tongue-tied with awe, but quick to make friends with Isabel's maid, recognising someone as neat and timid as herself.

When the luggage had been taken away and the servants had found their second-class carriage at the rear of the train, Deborah observed: 'That's not the girl I saw at the Priory, surely?'

'No,' said Isabel crossly. 'Miriam disappeared without a word a day or two after you left. She was there one afternoon, gone by morning. I always knew she was a flighty little baggage. But to take herself off just as we were preparing to set out on our journey — some of these girls have no sense of obligation, no gratitude.'

'You don't know where she went?'

'There was some young oaf in the village,' Justin contributed indifferently.

'Mother found me a new girl, the one you've seen. But I doubt she'll do. When we get back, I must make a more careful selection.'

'A paltry lot to choose from.' Justin looked out of the window as the train began to move.

Hour piled upon hour. Deborah began to recognise scattered landmarks and sketches of meadow. Here again were the rolling expanses, the dizzying sky and the hazy light along the rim of the world. She felt the stirring of apprehension such as she had experienced that first time.

Justin smiled across the compartment at her. 'You must see it as if you had never set eyes on it before.'

When the branch line train left the junction on its way to Ingmere, he reeled off a catalogue of the hillocks and coppices and sparse hamlets they passed. 'Dryford . . . Heathen's Covert, where that Neolithic grave was turned up a few years back . . . the end of Mockbeggar's Way . . . see the light on the bracken up there?' He identified warreners' huts and the dark heap of ash in the centre of what had been a gypsy encampment. 'Good thing for them they've moved on, or I'd have had a fancy to set the constable on 'em.' He pointed to a dark clump raised several feet above the scrub. 'Should be a fine lot of pheasant flushed out of there next month.' Sandall's cottage, Barkwell the tinker plodding his way across the heath: he was like her father, reciting the names of men who had served under him, a Welsh sergeant who had saved his life, devoted Indian servants who had come and gone but not been forgotten, all part of the warp and woof in which his own life was entwined.

By the time they reached Ingmere, Justin had contrived to make her feel that she was coming home. It was a perilously cosy feeling: she must not let herself succumb too readily.

They got down, laughing together, as the footman hurried from the back of the short train to hold the door open.

Deborah recognised the porter who had been here when she first set foot on this platform. Now he seemed almost an old friend. In the background was someone else she knew. General Fleming was getting painfully up into a carriage, helped by someone with his back to the new arrivals. Before Deborah could attract the general's attention, his attendant turned his head. It was Sir Randall Gaunt.

Intercepting her glance, Justin also looked along the platform. Then he came between the scene and Deborah, took her arm, and led her out on to the station approach.

'Where does the train go on to from here?' she asked.

'Yaddage.' He was curt. She had no idea whether Yaddage was a terminus, a junction, a town or a village.

There were several carriages outside the station, a busier sight than before. One began slowly to wheel round and away, having delivered its passengers to the train. Another creaked and grated on the cobbles as its two horses fidgeted and began to snap at each other.

Suddenly there came a boisterous shout. A tall young man with a brown felt wideawake set at a rakish angle on his head strode along the paving towards Justin, slapped him on the shoulder and then, retaining a light grip on his upper arm, insolently appraised Deborah.

Isabel made a little moue of annoyance, and when the young man addressed her with ironic politeness she turned towards their waiting coach with a perfunctory, 'Mr. Chevening.'

Justin introduced his friend as Harry Chevening. Chevening bowed over Deborah's hand, his fingers pressing through her glove. Where Justin's boldness was winning and boyish, Chevening's was impertinent. Deborah was glad to free herself and follow Isabel.

'Thetford Races?' she heard him say. Then a murmured colloquy, a brief laugh from Chevening and some vague protest from Justin; and 'Oh, that episode has been tidied up, never fear.'

As Justin was stooping to join them in the coach, a horse squealed angrily. There

144

was a burst of shouting, a cry, and the clatter of hoofs. From her window, Deborah caught a glimpse of one carriage swerving towards another and of two wheels grating together. A woman let out another cry, and from somewhere a child ran in front of a horse, and was thrown to one side. As she went down a wheel rolled forward and over her leg.

The scream bit into Deborah's breast. She put her hand briefly over her eyes, then made to follow Justin as he backed down from the coach and turned across the cobbles.

Harry Chevening's coachman was fighting to bring his horses to a standstill. Chevening himself lunged forward, then dodged as the nearer animal kicked wildly out. The coachman drove them straight at the wall on the far side of the approach, and brought them to a stop there, shuddering and sweating. As he slid from his box and calmed them, a woman bent sobbing over the girl crumpled in the middle of the approach.

Sir Randall Gaunt emerged from the station. Summing up the situation, he hurried towards the injured girl. The mother looked up uncertainly, trying to lift the child. 'Don't move her!' Gaunt snapped.

There was a moan from a group of people forming outside the inn. It rose to a howl. The woman tightened her grip around the child's shoulders and pulled her protectively closer.

'Let me see her,' said Gaunt.

The small crowd, as if prodded by some unseen hand, stumbled out onto the concourse and barred him from the mother and child. He went black with rage and raised his hand. Deborah thought he was going to strike them aside and force his way through. Then Chevening stepped forward.

'I think you're not needed here, Gaunt.'

'That leg! Can't you see it's important that immediate — '

'If it has to be sawn off,' said Chevening harshly, 'I shall personally ensure that it is sawn off swiftly and without fuss by a *qualified* surgeon.'

One of the women jeered. Gaunt

looked along their sullen faces, and then saw Deborah. As if furious that she should have witnessed his humiliation, he swung away and clambered into his coach. As he was driven away, someone in the crowd stooped and picked something up from near the palings. The coach turned down the side of the station approach and slowed before moving out on to the road. The man hurled his stone.

It cut a long, thin scar across the gleaming black paintwork and then bounced off onto the cobbles. It was a large oval eye stone.

8

Justin had promised that Deborah should see the breckland through his eyes. Whatever other intentions might underlie that promise, he quickly set about honouring it. Once or twice she wondered if this was a deliberate campaign, as well devised as his trip to Edinburgh, to lull her rather than sweep her off her feet. He would speak when he was ready; when he was sure that her defences had been persuasively undermined.

She warmed both to his tact and to his skill. At no time was it impossible for her to say that she had greatly enjoyed her stay and now must make preparations for returning to Edinburgh. But it grew daily a less desirable prospect. Justin was leading her, charming her, deeper and deeper into the landscape of his existence. The rules of the game were of his own devising, but she did not find them unfair or irksome. She would say yes or no as she chose, when she chose. In the meantime it was flattering that such a question should be implicit between them, and diverting to be the object of such attentions.

They walked, and rode; and it dawned on her that there was more to it than mere sight-seeing. When Justin guided her along paths that avoided the more cruelly harsh stretches of the breck underfoot, he carried with him a fowling-piece and unforcedly instructed her in its use. When she was smaller, she had sometimes been out after grouse with her father and a few friends, but had derived little enjoyment from it. Now she watched with reluctant admiration the deftness of his movements and the immediate response of his nerves and muscles to the slightest disturbance in the banks or scrub. He explained his responsibilities in administration of his land and of the game laws: they were things, it was tacitly implied, she would need to understand.

In the middle of a sentence, a hare bounded out from under their feet in a scatter of sand. Justin's gun swung up to his shoulder. When the hare was about thirty yards away, he murmured softly: 'Between the ears, I think.' The gun spoke, and there was the acrid smell of it across Deborah's nostrils. The hare took one last bound into the air, leaping convulsively over a bush that was not there, and then dropped.

As they walked towards it, a covey of partridge started from the bracken, disturbed by the shot. They started low, then formed a gently rising arc. Justin's head went back. He watched them as he reloaded, and then, in the most leisurely fashion, settled his gun into his shoulder and waited for the birds to wheel round. His left hand pulled steadily and gently round. Deborah did not want even one of the birds to die, yet she hung on his decision. Surely he had left it too late? They were rising, the angle was too accurate, he had lost them.

He fired. The leading bird seemed to rotate about its own beak, and then plunged to the earth a few yards from a clump of Scots pine. Justin let out a little sigh. When he turned triumphantly to her, she saw a thin line of moisture along his upper lip. His eyes narrowed as they had done when following his quarry. Deborah felt that she was full in his sights and he would soon bring her down.

He moved away to retrieve the fallen partridge. As he stooped over a stunted bramble bush, he stiffened. With wary fingers, he probed in and detached a twist of wire from the thorny branches. 'Setting snares!' He was quiet but frightening. 'We'll have the keeper set a few snares of his own hereabouts. And I'll see our friend gets his full seven years in Tasmania.'

While he showed her the countryside and taught her to recognise each feature of his domain, Lady Stannard drew her into the life of the household. Less purposeful than her son, she unashamedly enjoyed the tours of inspection for their own sake. Indoors she picked out relics of family history: the room used by Charles II when he brought one of his ladies over from Newmarket, the spinet at which Johann Christian Bach had composed music for performance when he returned to London, the room in which eight generations of Stannards had been born. In the gardens, a pergola covered by trailing creeper was known as the King's Walk after James I, who had strolled here during several visits from his hunting lodge at Thetford.

It struck Deborah that the distinguished names and colourful memories belonged largely to earlier centuries. The last few generations had withdrawn from the fashionable world, or had been discarded by it. Lady Stannard talked of staff problems and the heartbreak in trying to keep the gardens in reasonable condition. And then, with a little sideways glance, she would use a phrase such as 'You'll find out, my dear' or 'You may have different ideas' or 'If you want to know a little more', assuming that these were matters with which Deborah herself would soon be dealing.

'So dry this year.' They were on the terrace, looking down towards the stream, now only a trickle. 'I'm told some of the meres out on the breck are drying up. One day they'll find the bottom of the bottomless mere. Hasn't Justin told you about that? Oh, it's a gloomy place — always looks dark even when the sun shines on it, and folk tell stories of a brother and sister who were drowned there long ago . . . and then there's another tale about a mysterious face that stares out of the water and lures travellers into its depths.'

'I've heard similar tales,' said Deborah, 'in many parts of Europe.'

'Just so.' Now they were inside the house, exploring another corridor. 'We're most concerned, of course, about this drought. Everett tells me the well is giving trouble.' Her brow furrowed.

One end of the building was virtually sealed off, and in the west wing were locked doors and a number of half-landings that led nowhere. 'If we entertained more,' said Lady Stannard, 'or if there were children . . . ' She veered off to another subject. 'The difficulty of finding and keeping reliable staff! Of course we call on the estate families; they do owe us something. But they're so grudging, and so dismally incompetent.

Can't grasp the simplest thing — or won't. You'll see, my dear. But one really must not lower one's standards, must one, and anything you think advisable . . . '

On Sunday morning they drove together to church, and Deborah sat in the Stannard pew. All the servants not required to prepare lunch had followed and installed themselves, far behind, in pews at the back of the church. The Reverend Gerald Ormesby smiled radiantly at Deborah. Other heads from other pews turned towards her and then towards one another. She wished she could tell them that her presence here meant only that she was a guest at Stannard Priory. There were no further conclusions to be drawn; not yet.

As they left the church after service, a middle-aged woman with a black shawl over her head darted from the side of the churchyard path to pluck at Lady Stannard's arm. 'I'm sorry, m'lady, but I thought on't after what you said, and that it be no good marndering about, I do think I'd best speak out now.'

Lady Stannard wavered and slowed. Justin led Deborah and Isabel on a few paces and then looked impatiently back. Then he smiled, and moved closer to Deborah as the villagers straggled past. Some men touched their forelocks. The Stannard Priory servants filed past with military precision, each paying respects. It was in effect a rehearsal for the day when the banns were first called; and for the even greater ceremonial when Justin led her as his bride from the church to her new position as Lady Stannard of Stannard Priory.

'Mother's flock is, in my estimation, considerably larger than the rector's,' Justin was saying. 'And I fear she allows its members to bleat on for far too long.'

His contempt cut through the swell of her feelings for him. His impatience, she was learning, was often not far removed from callousness. She flinched from his zest for killing and hating: whether the target was a bird, an animal, a would-be poacher, or Randall Gaunt, he was swift to react and swift to destroy. Yet with this undisguised male savagery would go a zest for love so foreign to her that she dared not let herself think of it, but wanted to think of nothing else. She had lived, or half-lived, so long in the company of old age and illness. Justin's virile challenge was terrifying to accept, impossible to reject.

Lady Stannard rejoined them, fretful where her son would have been furious. 'I swear some of them are incapable of thinking twelve hours ahead. On impulse they say yes or no, and respectfully assure you they're honoured and obliged and goodness knows what else. And then they're off. I had asked a girl to come and be interviewed, to see if she would suit Isabel.'

'But Mother, the maid you found me is shaping up nicely.'

'A makeshift,' said Lady Stannard dismissively. 'I was never happy with the choice. I've been looking around for somebody more suitable, and I thought I'd found her, and now the mother says she has changed her mind and the girl can't come.'

'Why not?'

They walked to the gate and to the barouche waiting outside. Lady Stannard looked along the street and shook her head at the cottages and their occupants.

'All she would say was that the girl was used to working in the city, and had decided there were too many strange things going on about here and she was planning to go back. Yet only a day or two ago they were telling me she was unhappy in the city and wished to be nearer home.'

As Justin handed his mother into the barouche, Isabel asked: 'In these proceedings, was Miriam's name mentioned at all?'

Lady Stannard settled herself. 'I've no time for village gossip.' Then she crimped up her eyes. 'Oh, there was some talk about a young man who had jilted her, or she had jilted him. It is thought she ran off to London.'

'Where her career will be all too predictable,' said Justin.

★ ★ ★

Justin took Deborah and Isabel to Thetford Races. It was a warm day with no more than the faintest hint of autumn in the air. Isabel drew a fine veil down over her face as they set out, and tilted her ribbon-trimmed round hat against the dust and the sun.

Deborah had not been in this direction before, and while Isabel sank back and appeared to drowse she sat upright and alert, picking out now familiar landmarks from a different angle.

'Whatever is that?'

The coach was slowing for a tight turn at the crossroads. Close to the corner was a hummock topped by a little cairn of stones, with four larger pieces on the level ground, one at each corner.

'A grave.' Justin barely gave it a glance. 'Some girl who took her own life.'

In spite of the heat Isabel shivered, and slanted her hat against the lonely burial mound. Deborah turned to watch it recede. The four lumps at the corners were eye stones.

'I suppose,' Deborah ventured, 'those

stones are meant to keep evil away from the poor thing.'

'Or to keep her where she is,' said Justin.

'She hanged herself,' murmured Isabel, 'from — '

'Enough! We didn't bring Deborah back to the breckland in order to regale her with gloomy nonsense about unrequited love, or whatever it may have been.'

The road over the heath joined a wide turnpike and they bowled more swiftly down a long undulating hill towards the distant town.

The sight of the course and of other carriages swaying across the grass, the jolting and whinnying and the shouts of recognition between friends, awoke an instant response in Justin. As soon as Deborah's feet touched the ground, he unceremoniously seized her arm and hurried her into the densest part of the crowd. Within two or three minutes, she had been introduced to a number of effervescent young men whose names jumbled inextricably together in her head.

Isabel, protesting, struggled to avoid being separated from them by others elbowing through.

Greetings, guesses, snatches of information and misinformation were tossed to and fro. 'They're giving the Town Purse to six-year-olds this meeting, so that leaves poor old Humphreys high and dry . . . if the stewards are as sottish as they were during the spring meeting . . . ' Deborah found she had to cling to Justin. His head was close to hers, his eyes wide and greedy. In one roped-off corner, a dancing bear went through its paces. A few feet away, a juggler tried to distract the public's attention with a whirl of Indian clubs. Nobody could speak on a reasonable level. It was all shouting and incoherence.

They emerged from the crush nearer to the course itself. Costermongers were selling fruit from a line of barrows, and pedlars jabbed trays of pinchbeck jewellery at every passerby.

'I fear you'll find it all rather tame, Miss Ritchie.'

The intrusive voice drew a little gasp of

160

dismay from Isabel. As Harry Chevening bowed over Deborah's hand, she was aware from the corner of her eye of Isabel plucking at Justin's sleeve and shaking her head warningly.

'Harry.' There was wary pleasure in Justin's greeting.

'How shall we liven up these drab proceedings?'

'They seem vigorous and lively enough to me,' said Deborah.

'Ah, but you did not see our high days and holidays at their best. Remember the hang fairs, Justin?'

'Two only.'

'When we were boys, Miss Ritchie, people were not afraid to enjoy themselves.' Deborah looked away, not encouraging him to speak to her; but he continued brashly and with coarsening glee.

'I remember the last of the hang fairs. Three men to be executed in Gibbet Field — and a splendid departure they had of it! There were songs, and the ale flowed, and one of the rogues delivered a splendid last speech from the scaffold. Very gifted, some of them, in making long speeches before the bolt was drawn.' Chevening leaned towards Justin, his flushed features uncomfortably close to Deborah's, so that she could see the blue stubble on his chin and a little network of purplish veins that would better have befitted a much older man. 'With your influence, my dear fellow, why not revive the hang fairs? Let public executions be carried out with style once more, and let's all enjoy ourselves.'

'Such fashions are on the wane.'

'More shame on the world, then.'

Aware of Deborah's revulsion, Justin said to her: 'These were harsh things, but should not crime be harshly punished?'

'Not with mockery,' she said firmly. 'A man who faces his last moments — '

'Should do so in good company,' Chevening finished for her.

Deborah had hoped they could now break off the conversation and that Justin would lead her and his sister away. Instead, he fell into step with Chevening and they moved towards the paddock. 'Twenty minutes to the start of the subscription purse,' Chevening was

162

saying. 'Let's see what we fancy. You're prepared to bring us luck, Miss Ritchie?'

Isabel, trying to keep her manner light, said: 'Mr. Chevening, you'll finish by leading my brother into evil ways!'

'It needs no more than a twitch on the rein, Miss Stannard.'

Justin laughed uneasily, covering it by a mock snarl in the direction of a group of brightly painted gypsy caravans some yards away. Two men were laying out cards on a plank, apparently paying no heed to spectators loitering near. Two young women sold gingerbread and wooden pegs. An older one, dark-eyed and dark-lipped, sat on a three-legged stool offering bunches of herbs and sometimes bending attentively over an outstretched palm.

'Any of that pack who set foot on my land'll get short shrift,' growled Justin. 'The stewards ought not to let 'em near the course.'

The woman on the stool caught the lash of his tone and glanced up. It was Deborah she saw first, and she looked no farther. After a long stare, she tipped her stool back on one leg and said from the side of her mouth: 'That face bodes no good for you.'

The remark was addressed not to Deborah but to the nearer of the two men. His gaze followed hers and, like hers, was arrested. His expression reminded Deborah of Randall Gaunt's when they first met, asking where he could have seen her before.

The contact was so direct that she was on the verge of speaking. Then Justin said: 'What's that insolent lout staring at?' Rather than provoke an unpleasant scene, Deborah allowed Chevening to coax them all away towards the horses.

'And if we have a fancy,' said Chevening, 'let's not put money in the pockets of those scoundrels over there. Let us come to a private arrangement.'

Justin looked lovingly at the string of mounts plodding round within the rail. 'The chestnut,' he said.

'Done,' said Chevening. 'Fifty?'

Justin glanced at his sister; and markedly did not glance at Deborah. His

tongue dabbed at his upper lip. He said:
'Ten.'

'My dear fellow . . . ' Chevening gave
an exaggerated sigh. 'Oh, yes, I see. But of
course. Miss Ritchie, what a benevolent
influence you wield! To cure him so
quickly!'

Justin stiffened. 'If you don't wish to
wager ten — '

'Guineas?'

'Naturally.'

'If that is the best we can do, then let's
settle for it.'

As the two men watched the horses
lining up for the off, Isabel pressed
affectionately against Deborah in the
crush. 'I was sure,' she said. 'From the
moment we met, I've been sure.'

There was a yell as the race began.
Justin's hand was clenched on the rail.
His whole being was concentrated on the
chestnut as it pulled up to third place,
gained, then fell back to fourth. He willed
it to force its way forward again, spurred
and whipped it with his mind . . .

When it lost, his fingers went limp and
there was a husky scrape in his throat.

'Now, to recoup,' said Chevening, 'you'll have to double. Clear your loss and put yourself ahead. Or if you'd prefer it, we can go into partnership for the next race, select one of the less scoundrelly touts — '

'I'll lick my wound for a while,' said Justin. Moving as close to Deborah as Isabel had been, he added: 'I fancy the ladies are in need of refreshment.'

As they edged their way to the refreshment marquee, Deborah sensed that the boisterous shouts and solicitations from all sides were as much music in Justin's ears as the fiddles scraping away within a dancing booth. But he applied himself to her and Isabel, talking to dampen down the temptations that reached out to him,

Chevening crossed and re-crossed their path throughout the afternoon. Twice he tried to lure Justin back to the course, and the third time succeeded.

'A small flutter to round off the event?' Unwilling to accept defeat, Chevening was now more provocative, daring Justin to assert himself.

Justin's head turned to follow the gleaming flank of a roan. The fever burned within him.

Chevening said: 'It's called Sir Walter. A good Scottish omen, wouldn't you say, Miss Ritchie?'

Justin could not resist. 'A fiver in a good cause?' he entreated her. 'In memory of our strolls along Princes Street, shall we say?'

There was the same utter absorption as the horses thundered forward; the same tightening of mouth and muscle; the same scratching sound in his throat when the horse faltered; and then a jubilant whoop as it pulled forward and won by a length.

'You brought me luck. I knew it.'

'And when the luck is running,' Chevening insinuated, 'it would be damnable ingratitude to falter. Last race of the day: bestow your blessing on it.'

Justin shook his head.

Chevening derisively imitated the movement. 'Miss Ritchie, I'm astounded. He does intend to make the purest impression on you.' The awed tone was laced with malice. 'A pity your late lamented brother-in-law didn't have the benefit of your guidance. He, alas, never knew when to stop.'

Justin said: 'I think we should leave before we're caught in the general exodus.'

Glancing back once as they made their way to the carriage, Deborah saw Chevening planted immovably where they had left him, watching their departure.

★   ★   ★

They dined late that evening, with dusk a deepening mauve tinge along the terrace and in the oak trees. Night was held at bay by two candelabra in the centre of the table, each shaped as a nymph holding aloft a spray of gilded branches. Deborah had changed into her green crinoline and deeply pointed bodice, with deep revers revealing the little spattering of freckles which the day's sun had dabbed across her bosom. Justin appeared in a blue dress coat with a white satin waistcoat. As they sat down at table Lady Stannard and Isabel exchanged conspiratorial smiles.

Deborah's heart quickened. She knew there was something in the air, and all at once felt dizzy with uncertainty. She was not ready for it. Lady Stannard made an arch joke about men forever remaining irresponsible boys at heart; and Isabel talked about some woman Deborah could not recall having even noticed. Justin laughed, warm glints in his eyes reflecting dancing candle flames. He looked long and solemnly at Deborah, and she could not look away.

She was the only one to strike a discordant note. Drowsy from the day's tumult and journeying, and from the claret glowing in her glass, it was jarred from her: 'What did Mr. Chevening mean about Edwin, and not knowing when to stop?'

'Anything Mr. Chevening may have said about anybody at all,' Lady Stannard retorted, 'would be worth neither repeating nor considering.'

After the meal, Deborah was caught up again in the pulsing rhythm of that dance she had felt before. Lady Stannard and Isabel were stepping backwards, leaving

Justin to complete the figure with her.

He led her down the terrace steps to the grass. The evening chill on her arms was welcome. Stars were a thousand bright sequins across the velvet of the sky. Their light softened the shadows under the trees, seeming to draw a faint answering light from the earth itself.

'You no longer feel a stranger here, I think?'

'No guest was ever more gently acclimatised,' she said.

'A guest? To me,' said Justin, 'you already belong here.'

Their steps took them beside the bank of the trickling stream. As her eyes grew more accustomed to the dark, she could make out each contorted pinnacle of the priory ruins, and a white smear down the edge of the moat. The whiteness took on recognisable outlines as she studied it.

'But that's a boat,' she said. 'Lady Stannard said nobody was allowed across to the ruins, ever.'

'Rubble has to be cleared away from time to time. And the creeper has to be trimmed back when its weight becomes too dangerous.'

A nightingale raised its fluting voice. Justin was silent. He was not so much summoning up courage to speak as allowing the atmosphere to cast its own spell upon her. He had no wish to talk about the ruins or any other practical matter concerning the estate.

There was a distant thrumming. She put her hand to her breast, feeling the throb of it through her fingertips.

'Deborah. You know well what it is I have to ask you.'

But the sound came nearer, and was not the pulse of her heart but an urgent thudding of hoofs straight out of the breck, racing over the far ridge and down towards the opposite bank of the stream. Justin swore incredulously, uncontrollably.

The leading horseman of three reined in, twitched his cape back over his shoulder, and cried: 'Good evening to you. Instructing Miss Ritchie in the niceties of the pleasure pavilions?'

Harry Chevening's drunken splutter

dissolved into a long, senseless laugh.

Justin said: 'This is a strange short cut for you to be taking.'

'A short cut to a few more hours of good talk ... a hand of cards, d'you think? ... a glass to settle the stomach.'

'It's late,' said Justin furiously.

'Not unwarrantably so. We have sat up later than this, you and I. All of us, eh?'

His two companions added their befuddled laughs.

Justin took Deborah's arm. 'I think it is time we went indoors.'

'We'll escort you,' shouted Chevening. 'See you come to no harm.' He set his horse to leap the stream, and the others blundered in pursuit. 'And then drink to clear our heads.'

'You seem to have drunk well already.'

'And eaten.' Chevening set his black mare to trot beside them. 'The wrong proportions, I fear. I am suffering from a sanguineous congestion.'

'A vigorous gallop would clear your head.'

Chevening ignored the hint. As Justin and Deborah continued up the slope, the riders formed a little procession in their wake, sniggering and saying 'Hush, hush!' at intervals.

Justin drew Deborah farther ahead. 'I cannot very well turn them away without some brief hospitality.'

She could see no reason why not, other than a fear that they might attack him. But she did not think cowardice was numbered among Justin's failings.

Lady Stannard was dismayed when the visitors' clattered into the hall. Chevening gave her a sweeping bow. As Justin said, with false heartiness, 'Just a night-cap in the library to speed you on your way,' she tried to take him aside.

'I had hoped that at least for a while, until you had accomplished . . . '

But Deborah was only a few feet away, and Chevening swaggered closer; and the words trailed away.

Deborah fought back a yawn. 'If you will excuse me, I think I should retire.'

'We'd all do well to follow your example,' said Lady Stannard shakily.

Justin hesitated to declare even now what had been on the tip of his tongue such a short while ago. But his mother had tugged the bell-pull. A footman brought candlesticks, and Kirstie Hamilton took one to light Deborah up the stairs. Chevening eyed the girl with frank lasciviousness as she bobbed past him. The butler despatched another footman to the cellar to fetch a number of bottles for the gentlemen. The brief hospitality showed signs of being protracted.

As Kirstie brushed her hair with slow, soothing strokes, Deborah looked at the girl's preoccupied face in the glass. 'I hope you're comfortable here, Kirstie.'

'They're unco' strange, the way they talk below stairs, miss.' The girl sounded pleased. And when Deborah dismissed her for the night and, opening the bedroom door, she let in a faint burst of laughter and the thud of another door in the distance, she added with self-satisfied primness: 'And there's nowhere nearly enough to keep a body properly occupied.'

'But you like it well enough?'

'Oh, aye, I like it fine, miss, thank you.'

The room was oppressively warm.

Deborah opened the window and leaned out. The eerie half-light of the stars touched unexpected edges and died away into ragged lakes of gloom. For the first time she realised that what she had taken to be a misshapen branch was in fact the brittle claw of the ruined priory window crooked against the sky.

She lay in bed listening to the secret rustlings and stirrings of the night. She must have slept and then woken again. Voices of revellers cut through the shreds of a dream. The men must have come out of the library on to the far end of the terrace.

'Well, I'm shocked . . . it won't do at all,' Harry Chevening slurred. 'Edwin, now, *Edwin* knew what a debt of honour . . . '

'Keep your voice down, man.'

'Oho. We're a reformed character, are we not? Well, give you time, eh?' Footsteps scuffed along the terrace. 'But when it comes to it, we know what a real wager would be. That's a stake I'll accept, gladly.'

'Bottle's empty,' said one of the men.

They mumbled back indoors, leaving only the wisp of an incomprehensible taunt from Chevening: 'Keep it in the family, eh?'

9

Justin led her out on to the terrace when the morning was still fresh.

'Deborah, we were unpardonably interrupted last evening.'

His eyes were lacklustre and his usual overflowing energy had been drained from him. He still carried the faint staleness of wine and tobacco about him. But his voice was steady and determined. Somehow she did not want him to speak. Last evening all might have been well. This morning she felt a lingering distaste; wanted a postponement until she could be sure of him and sure of herself.

She parried: 'You seemed very ready to pardon the interruption.'

'I am sorry. I was taken unawares.'

'I gained the impression that such visitations were not uncommon.'

With a flash of his old fire, he said: 'My friends have livened up many a dismal evening. If they overreach themselves occasionally, that means no lasting harm. If you wish them to keep their distance in future, I will see to it.'

'What have my wishes to do with it?'

Justin took her right hand in his, and let his left hand slide gently on to her wrist. 'They have everything to do with it, and with so much else besides.' He looked deep into her eyes as he asked: 'Deborah, will you be my wife?'

She ought to have been able to yield then, as he demanded. What right had she to stay in this house if she were not prepared to accept the proposal which she had known would come? It had grown more sonorous with every passing hour. She had not repudiated it; had been demurely awaiting it.

All she could say was: 'You do me a great honour.'

'And you will accept?'

His urgency was disquieting. A lover's impatience? If it had been so, her response would surely have been instinctively right. Last night's cloud still hung above the terrace. She faltered: 'I . . . there have been so many decisions for me to make these last months . . . this is the most serious of them all.'

'You cannot have been unaware that you would have to make it.'

'I need time to consider, sir.'

'I have become 'sir'?'

'Justin,' she said, 'you must leave me to myself for a while.'

He released her hand. 'Of course. I'm a boor. There are delicacies in this matter — little feints and withdrawals, a proper hesitation before surrender, yes?'

'I would not have you think I'm trifling with you.'

'No.' He leaned on the balustrade and looked away from her, over the disciplined landscape created for his ancestors and himself. Deborah wondered if he were conjuring up a picture of his own children playing on the green slope, hiding and romping among the trees. She had an impulse to reach out and touch him; but the time was not yet. 'Very well,' he said. 'I'll leave you to ponder it. Will an hour be enough — two, three? It's a most agreeable morning: walk where you choose, and I'll ensure that you're not disturbed. But Deborah . . . I entreat you, persuade yourself towards me and not away from me. I want you for my wife. I want you to be as sure as I am.'

Through one of the tall windows, she noticed a ghostly blur of figures moving together and apart, beyond the glass. As Justin turned towards the casement door at the end, his mother appeared in the opening. 'I've just told Palgrave you're not to be interrupted.' Lady Stannard glanced hopefully towards Deborah. 'But you've finished?'

'We've . . . ah . . . postponed our discussion for a little while. I can do with an hour or two's distraction. Don't skulk behind the curtains, Palgrave. What's it about?'

A man in high buttoned gaiters, the capacious pockets of his tweed jacket sagging as though from constant misuse, took an apologetic step out into the light. 'Two poachers, m'lord. One of 'em got caught up in the covert by Blacktoft trapping banks, and t'other was trying to get him loose when we spotted 'un.'

Justin brightened. 'Good for you, Palgrave. You've got them safe?'

'One's got a right old mess of an ankle, from the trap.'

Deborah burst out: 'A trap? But surely they're not — '

'We have one or two comparatively harmless little devices of our own,' said Justin. 'We don't *invite* men to walk into them — and if a man's not in the covert in the first place, he won't do so, will he?' His step was springy as he joined Palgrave. 'I'll come with you. On your oath and mine, we'll have them committed to Yaddage lock-up.'

In the doorway, he looked back at Deborah for an intent moment.

She felt that he would enjoy committing the poor felons into imprisonment as keenly as hearing her expected reply later in the day.

* * *

Deborah took a leisurely stroll down to the stream, her head bent, and then tried to shock herself into a decision by spinning abruptly round and looking full at the house.

She was being asked to become Lady Stannard, of Stannard Priory in the County of Norfolk. It had an attractive ring to it. Lady Stannard was obviously prepared to hand over the reins of the household to her. With some encouragement, and with as much of her money as he chose to use, Justin could develop the estate. They could keep on the house in Edinburgh, visit when they liked; and perhaps the Stannards already had a place in London . . .

It would be so easy to surrender, to allow herself to *belong*.

What would her father have made of Justin? What would his advice would have been? There could be no answer from beyond the grave. And her father, really, though relying so much on her, had never seen her truly as a young woman. The distinction between his little girl and his efficient companion had always been hazy in his mind.

The decision must be hers and hers alone.

Did she love him?

She knew her father, Mr. MacKenzie, and all the family friends she had mixed with at various periods during her life would have regarded that question as frivolous. Was it an advantageous marriage? That came first. If she could truthfully say she respected the man who had offered her his hand, that she believed they could agree and be comfortable together, and that their children would be well provided for, the contract should surely be signed. With proper investment of one's assets, love might come as a lucky dividend.

Deborah walked back up the slope, concentrating on seeing herself as mistress of Stannard Priory; but catching instead tantalising glimpses of Justin as a bewitching, dazzling stranger in Edinburgh. Here he was too much in control. Yet was that not what she wanted? She had led for too long. It was time for her to be guided; ordered, even.

Mid-morning tea was sent out to the terrace on a tray, with a plate of thin biscuits. She was being treated, she thought, as an invalid. The silence was unnatural. Lady Stannard was perhaps tip-toeing along corridors in order not to disturb her.

I love him, thought Deborah and fiercely. *I wish to be his wife and we shall be happy.* He would take her hand again, and this time there would be no interruptions and no doubts. He would ask the question again and she would say yes. After that, everything would be so sweet and uncomplicated.

So how was it that even in the secret resonances of her own head, she could not hear herself saying yes?

She paced round the end of the house. A gardener edged deferentially back behind a yew hedge whose bird shapes he had been carefully trimming. She was alone, her mind an unhelpful blank.

A carriage emerged from the lime avenue and swung to a halt under the brick gateway. She recognised coach and coachman. They came from Saxwold Hall.

As the coachman got down and approached the three steps to the entrance, carrying an envelope, the butler appeared in the doorway. At the same moment, Lady Stannard hurried round the house from the far side. Had she been spying on her, watching her expression and her movements in the hope of guessing at a decision?

She took the letter from the coachman before the butler could intervene, frowned at it, and was about to go indoors when the coachman saw Deborah.

'Isn't this the lady?'

Lady Stannard turned and held out the letter reluctantly. It was addressed to Miss Ritchie. In it, Sir Randall Gaunt asked if she could possibly come to lunch that day. General Fleming particularly wished to round off details of the memorial they had planned for his son and daughter-in-law, but was not well enough to make the journey along the rough breck roads. The coachman would wait for her. If she could not manage today at such short notice, for which he apologised, perhaps she would be kind enough to send a reply indicating a time which would suit her.

But let it be within a day or two, as General Fleming must soon return to Bath.

Deborah had no wish to visit Randall Gaunt again, but she felt a close sympathy with the old soldier and would hate to seem discourteous to him.

Her mind was made up for her by Lady Stannard, who waited to be told what was in the letter and said at once: 'Most unsuitable. Of course you won't think of going.'

'It will save a great deal of correspondence later.'

'I'm quite sure Justin would forbid it if he were here.'

The coachman and butler stepped a few discreet paces back.

Deborah said: 'I am not yet Lord Stannard's chattel.'

The two stared at each other. Lady Stannard's gaze was the first to fall; the older woman was desperately afraid of putting a foot wrong, either with her son or with Deborah.

'To send for you like this, out of the blue,' she grumbled after a pause, 'expecting you to dash off at his command!'

'When I first came here,' Deborah said, 'Justin and Isabel spirited me away from Saxwold Hall with scant ceremony. It may amuse Sir Randall to emulate them.'

'It doesn't amuse *me*.' Lady Stannard fidgeted. 'Oh, very well, if you must go, I'll send the carriage to bring you back.'

'I'm sure Sir Randall will make arrangements — '

'I should prefer that he did not. Draper will call for you at half past three sharp. That will allow you ample time to discuss your business.'

Having established her independence, Deborah conceded this point.

Kirstie was summoned to accompany her, and within fifteen minutes they were setting out. The skilful driver maintained a brisk pace without ever subjecting them to the fierce jolts and skids which were too common a feature of these rutted roads.

Meeting Randall Gaunt again, she felt stiff and unsure of herself. He strode out to meet her with what she thought was dour condemnation in his eyes. His handshake was brief.

'I was surprised,' she said as they went towards the study, 'to learn that General Fleming was staying with you.'

'And I was surprised to find that you had returned to stay with the Stannards.'

The general sat near the window with a rug over his knees. Since they had last met, his flesh seemed to have shrivelled. Skeletal jaw and fingers provided an all too fitting accompaniment to the anatomical chart she had seen on her first visit. Her extended hand was trembling. But his smile was so warm and genuinely welcoming that in his company she relaxed.

'We don't want to keep you too long away from your friends, Miss Ritchie,' said Gaunt. 'I shall have lunch served the moment you are ready.'

Deborah went upstairs with Kirstie. In that small room where she had found Beatrice's brooch, she wondered whether to confront Gaunt with the evidence, but dismissed the idea of causing an unpleasant scene before the dignified,

188

likeable old man.

When she went downstairs again, General Fleming was trying to push himself up from his chair. Instinctively Deborah put one arm round his shoulder, and took his weight as he staggered upright. Slowly they made their way together to the dining-room. Ageless and unfathomable, Lady Gaunt looked down upon the table.

'Now, m'dear,' the general wheezed, 'not expecting to see me still in these parts, hm? Went to London — a number of dismal matters to tidy up. Then young Gaunt asked me back here . . . '

Sir Randall — young? Yet of course he was. For all his forbidding appearance, he was a vigorous, powerful man in his thirties with a clear if dark, gaze; and as great an assurance as Justin. But no warmth — none that he would show.

'Known one another for years,' Fleming was nodding on. 'Mutual friends, you know — army surgeon, splendid fellow, you'd have loved him — and that's how Edwin came to lease Toft Warren House.'

'Not the happiest outcome of a friendship,' said Gaunt.

'My dear fellow, you're hardly going to blame yourself for *that*?' The general's eyes were bright as he turned towards Deborah. 'Trouble with *this* one is, he tries to shoulder too many responsibilities. Drives himself too hard.'

Gaunt glared down at his plate. 'Whatever you decide about the memorial, please be assured that I'm prepared to deal with any minor snags in your absence. I assume you'll both be many miles away before long. Keep me informed, and I'll keep an eye on progress.'

'Won't be a nuisance to you more than another day or two,' said General Fleming.

They waited for Deborah to speak.

She said: 'I . . . I may be here for longer than I originally intended.'

'I see,' said Gaunt.

He made no further contribution to the conversation, letting his two guests exchange views on the final form of the memorial. Fleming explained that he had gone to Yaddage, a town farther up the branch line, to pay a deposit on some stone which the dealer was unwilling to supply to the remote breckland mason without some surety. Did Miss Ritchie have any preference regarding the wording? And dates and suchlike — in English or Latin? They were points she had hardly considered, but she realised that the local craftsmen could scarcely be left to go their own sweet way.

Though Randall Gaunt was offering no comment, she became aware of a brief little movement, a glance, a disturbing attentiveness. It was as though he listened not to her words but to something beyond which only he could hear. When he passed her the salt cellar, and their fingers brushed together Deborah wondered if, once, he had looked at Beatrice as he now looked at her.

At the end of the meal he said: 'I will have coffee sent to you both in the study, and then promise you will be left in peace for as long as you require.'

'A carriage is coming for me at half past three,' said Deborah.

'But I had every intention of returning you in — '

'Lady Stannard insisted. She did not wish you to be put out any further.'

'I'm an infernal nuisance,' growled Fleming.

Silently Randall Gaunt took the general's left arm, while Deborah took his right, and they returned to the study. There Gaunt left them.

There was little left to discuss now. The practical details were settled. They went over them once more, and sipped their coffee. The general's rug slid from his knees to the floor. He shivered as Deborah picked it up.

'It's a cold house,' she said.

'It's my old bones, not the house.'

'Cold,' she repeated, 'and unlived-in.'

'It has lacked the warmth of a woman's presence for too long.'

'Sir Randall never wished to remarry? Or,' said Deborah recklessly, 'no eligible young woman cared to commit herself to this . . . this atmosphere?'

'What do you mean by that?' His fierceness rattled the cup and saucer in her hand. He was like an emaciated old terrier.

'It's a cold house. And it always will be.'

'Rubbish. It wasn't always so, and it doesn't have to go on being so. Randall's fault, I'll grant you. Shutting himself away into an obsession with work so that he has no time to think of anything else — damned unhealthy. Needs someone to restore him to life, give him a new purpose.'

'Nobody has tried?'

'I've no idea. Haven't seen him for ages, till this wretched business. But he doesn't seem to have changed his ways. And the slanders get worse. Ignorant rabble!'

Deborah leaned forward to take his cup and saucer from the table beside him before they met with some disaster.

He barked at her again. 'I suppose you believe he killed his wife?'

'I don't know what to — '

'But you've heard the talk and I'll be bound you half believe it. Listen to me, young woman! Randall Gaunt didn't kill his wife or egg anyone else on to kill her. He was only on the threshold of his medical career at the time, and it wouldn't have been ethical for him to operate on his own wife. People's memories are pretty unreliable stuff, y'know. Get facts and dates confused, and have faulty recollections.'

This was true enough. Deborah thought back to her father's confusion regarding dates of campaigns in which he had fought, of his confusion between her birthday and Beatrice's, and of places they had been in a month or a year before.

'Elizabeth Gaunt had a tumour,' the general harangued her. 'They did their best to save her, but the operation went on too long. Too painful. Gaunt had to watch it. Wanted to be with her, wanted to believe she'd pull through. When she gave up, I've heard it said that his friends feared for his reason. And that's another story that may have been twisted, since. But one thing you may depend on: it was Lady Gaunt's death that turned Gaunt's career into a vocation. He went into a rage, and it's my opinion it was the rage that saved him. No succumbing to despair for Gaunt. Instead he went after the enemy that had destroyed his wife. Devoted himself to surgery. And to relieving pain. Pain's a murderer more often than the injury itself. Seen it in the field too damned often.

'Gaunt's been looking for ways of giving a surgeon time to work instead of being just a fast-moving butcher. All his own money ploughed not into his estates but into research. Some folk know in their bones he's right. Some of them creep here at night for help — all the way from the villages, rather than call in their own doctor. And then there's the others. The others — the rabble,' bellowed Fleming, 'and the jealous HQ staff of his own profession.'

'According to their own lights,' Deborah ventured, 'they must have had reasons.'

'Lights? Liver and lights! Because he stood by a physician who was trying to find a safer anaesthetic, and because surgeons aren't supposed to speak to mere physicians if they can help it, let alone work with them as equals — *that's* why he was struck off. Hmph! About as good at working together, these doctors and surgeons, as the horse artillery and a regiment of foot.'

It was almost half past three. Through the window, Deborah caught the gleam of a carriage turning in through the distant gates and making its way up the drive.

General Fleming, exhausted by his outburst, apologised for not accompanying her to the coach. Randall Gaunt reappeared and silently escorted her out. In the hall Boynton was waiting to open the door. His master waved him away.

'Miss Ritchie.' There was an urgent pulse in his voice which seemed to communicate itself to her fingers as they shook hands. 'If you ever need my assistance, I trust you won't hesitate to get in touch with me.'

'You're very kind, sir.'

His hand still grasped hers, its touch no longer chill. 'I'm not speaking merely of your gift to the church, or such things. At any time, whatever happens, I want you to turn first to me.'

When his hand released hers, he was still in some way holding her: his eyes would not let her go, he had more to say and she waited for him to speak without knowing why she should listen.

He said: 'When you have changed your mind, no matter how difficult and how late it may seem — '

'Change my mind, sir? About what?'

'I don't need to be a thought-reader to know the offer that has been made to you. Or will be made any day now.'

'You have no right — '

'No, I have no right. But I cannot remain silent. I should have spoken sooner, but it seemed *too* soon. I could not let myself believe what I saw — and felt. My blind preoccupation with work . . . I'm unused to trusting feelings when I've mistrusted them so long. Miss Ritchie — Deborah.' He made her name a cry of pain. His hands gripped her shoulders and forced her round to face him. 'You have made me see, and feel. You must hear me, before it's too late.'

She slid away from him and wrenched

the heavy door open, not looking back, fleeing from the dark aura of his presence into the carriage.

Kirstie was already waiting beside it. She blinked wonderingly at her mistress. On the journey towards Stannard Priory, she stared steadily out of the window at the sand, the pitted ridges, and the population of thousands upon thousands of flints, twisted into inhuman shapes and polished by the windblown sand.

Deborah looked out but saw little: saw only the set of Justin's head as he waited for her reply. Then, a watchful and growing insistent figure behind him: Randall Gaunt. General Fleming had spoken out for Gaunt. But, old and ailing, had he not fallen too readily under Sir Randall's powerful spell? Even if everything he had said were true, might it not also be true that Sir Randall was so wedded to his work — blindly preoccupied, on his own admission — that the human heart and the human body had ceased to mean anything other than raw material for his own use?

It was the kind of argument Justin

would have advanced and would wish her to accept. But it no longer fitted what her senses told her about Randall Gaunt. Her mind tried to assert itself over those perilous senses, but they throbbed and swayed in conflict with her thoughts and the sway of the carriage.

* * *

The carriage wheels jolted to a halt on the verge. Deborah lowered the window and put her head out. There was nothing approaching from the opposite direction.

'What is it, Draper?'

'Somethin' a bit queer over yonder, miss. On the bottomless mere. When we get home, I'd best send someone over to have a look — or send word back to Sir Randall Gaunt, bein' as it's on his land.'

'Just a moment.'

Deborah was fascinated by the notion of the bottomless mere. She stepped down, but could see nothing.

The coachman pointed. 'From up here I can see over the bank, miss. Never known the level go down out of sight like that.'

Treading cautiously, Deborah picked her way across the treacherous ground, watchful for sharp flints that might turn her foot and her ankle. The coachman got down, and Kirstie came hurrying after.

The mere came into sight round the end of a shallow ridge of furze. It was about thirty or forty feet across, with a ragged lip like that of some extinct volcano. As Deborah approached, she expected to see eventually the edge of the water. But the bank continued to shelve down, and from a slight knoll she saw what had attracted the coachman's attention. Something white, slimed with weed, seemed to grope up the bank.

'I think you'd best wait, miss.' Draper quickened his pace and passed her.

Deborah ignored him, and did not stop until she was at the edge of the mere. The old legend was absurd. It was far from bottomless: not even unusually deep. All the water had drained away, leaving a saucer-shaped depression coated with green and yellow mud, already drying out. Spread-eagled against the far slope of the basin was the naked body of a girl.

'Kirstie, go back to the carriage and wait there.'

'But, miss — '

'Go back.'

The coachman slid gingerly down the slope to the corpse. Each wrist and ankle had been weighted by a large eye stone, secured by rope passing through the hole. The girl must have been lowered or tossed in face down, and had come to rest against the lower curve of the bank, half-embedded in mud. Below trailers of green slime, her puffy white back had a pattern of weals that could have been dug into the flesh by a whip, or a knife — or a scalpel.

Draper hesitated, then stooped and tried to move the head. It came free with a patter of dried and flaking mud. He turned the head carefully.

Water and mud had not had time to do their worst. The girl's face was still easily recognisable. It was the face of Miriam, Isabel Stannard's lost maid.

10

Lady Stannard and Isabel accompanied Deborah solicitously upstairs, afraid she might faint if left to make the journey on her own. Deborah took cowardly advantage of their conventional reaction. After the first dizziness of identifying the pallid corpse, a swift longing to be sick and then a determination not to be, she had been in no danger of collapse. But she was glad of the excuse to lie down and be left alone; glad to postpone the moment when Justin would once more ask his question.

Justin had come striding out onto the steps as they approached Stannard Priory. He wrenched open the door of the carriage before it had even stopped, and before a footman could hurry from the house. His rage was all too apparent. When the coachman jumped down and tried to report what they had found in the mere, Justin brushed him aside. Deborah realised that he was preparing to berate her for having visited Saxwold Hall when she should have been giving serious and uninterrupted thought to his proposal.

Before he could speak, she said: 'There is a dead woman lying out on the breck. I do not think she should be left exposed there.'

'A dead woman? What story is this that you've brought back from your — '

'Miriam,' said Deborah. 'Your sister's maid. She's in what I believe you all call the bottomless mere.'

His face went as white as hers must have been when she realised whose the pitiful corpse was. Anger died as the blood ebbed from his cheeks; and then, inexplicably, blazed up again. 'Miriam?' It was incredulous and venomous. He spun towards the coachman, ready to listen now. 'What the devil is this all about?'

In the blessed isolation of her room, Deborah was intermittently aware of comings and goings. She imagined someone being sent to remove the body from the dried-up mere; then tried not to imagine it in too much detail. Police must surely be notified, the coroner would find himself with another inquest on his hands, Justin would presumably initiate inquiries of some kind, was perhaps riding off at this moment in some official capacity . . .

Kirstie brought her a light supper on a tray. The girl tried to maintain a funereal manner, but was too chirpy to sustain it. It was all so dreadful and exciting. Clearly the whole place had livened up. 'His lordship's in such a state, miss! Sending folk off here, there and everywhere. I wouldnae like to be crossing him in anything this night.' She giggled admiringly, then adopted a hushed but still eager tone. 'What would ye suppose that poor wee girl got herself into, then? Coming from this very house, too.'

Deborah calmed her as well as she could and sent her away. Justin's responses seemed as exaggerated as so many of his moods and gestures, she thought ruefully. Life with him would always be subject to these outbursts and violent swings of humour. It might be stimulating, or exhausting. She was not frightened by such a prospect, but wondered about the deeper source of his tempers.

At least his wholehearted concentration on this present drama kept him away from her. In the morning when she came down, to be met by a dazed but still gently sympathetic Lady Stannard, he had already left.

'That poor wretched child.' Lady Stannard groaned. 'Whatever folly could have led her to such an end?' Like Kirstie, she assumed that Miriam's tragedy was largely of her own making.

'Her murderer is presumably some local man,' said Deborah.

'I hate to even think of it. Such a terrible thing. But they are such savages.'

'A local girl, a local setting, and one of your local charms, too: the eye stones. They brought poor Miriam little luck.'

'I gather you are fully recovered,' said Lady Stannard with some asperity. 'For myself, I find I prefer not to pursue such horrors. They're best left to those whose duty it is to deal with them.'

Justin returned and reported his actions. The parish constable had been sent out with his instructions. The girl's parents had been notified. Sir Randall Gaunt, on whose land the mere lay, had been notified. The inquest was set. Isabel must attend, since Miriam had been her personal maid and the coroner would wish to ask a few routine questions. Deborah, however, could be spared this further ordeal: the coachman's evidence would be sufficient to cover the finding of the body.

'But as I was there, I feel I should attend also.'

'While I,' said Justin, 'would prefer you to stay at home and give earnest thought to that other, far more important matter.'

'I have given it thought.'

'Ah.' He slapped his hip. 'And you have decided — '

'I would sooner we spoke of it at a more appropriate time.'

'When there is no longer death in the air?' He was in a great good humour, immersed in a score of things at once, sure of himself — too sure to have any doubts. 'You're right, of course. We'll get this out of the way. And then we shall talk.'

★   ★   ★

The inquest was held in a back room of the Stannard Arms in Meddleheath. It was not a large room, and this day could only accommodate those persons whose duty it was to be there. Eight jurors appointed by the coroner were self-conscious in their Sunday best. There was a smell of leather and warm, sweaty serge; and of sour ale. Two cane-seated chairs were set against one wall for Deborah and Isabel. For other witnesses there was a wooden bench, but only the dead girl's parents and the coachman used it. Justin leaned against the wall beside the coroner's table. Randall Gaunt stood on the far side of the room with one thumb hooked into his waistcoat pocket. He stood motionless, quite detached from everyone else in spite of the limited space, looking out impassively over the heads of the others: looking more often than not, Deborah soon realised, at herself.

She turned her head, making a pretence of studying a notice fastened to the wall beside her. It proclaimed the existence of the Ingmere Association, formed by the nobility and gentry of ten parishes and pledging for the public weal a tariff of rewards for information on burglaries, stealing or maiming livestock, poaching, setting fire to goods or property, and for criminal assault or murder, and the assurance that the tracking down and prosecution of offenders would be most rigorously administered by the association and such officers as it chose to appoint.

Deborah caught Isabel's eye. 'Another of Justin's chores,' said Isabel. 'You'll have to accustom yourself to . . . ' She left it incomplete, but the arch invitation to let slip a confidence was unmistakable.

Deborah said: 'Have you no police force here, then?'

'Police?' Isabel laughed. 'The county endorses the new acts, yes. And towns are being compelled to follow suit. But they have not yet made themselves felt here. The parish constable still needs the backing of a local prosecuting society.'

She was about to say more, but the coroner came in and took his place.

Dr. Abbott's wispy silver hair straggled down behind the ears, and behind spectacles his eyes were restless, matching the fidgeting, tapping fingers of his left hand. He wore a high, hard white collar that forced his head several degrees backwards; but when he saw Sir Randall Gaunt he managed to force his chin down so that he could look at the table for the greater part of the time.

The coroner had a voice like a wandering bee, buzzing in fits and starts, sharp one second and then droning off into unintelligibility the next. Whenever he glanced at Justin Stannard, the pitch rose and he tended to gabble.

Discovery of the corpse was described by Draper, the coachman, and confirmed by Deborah. Although Justin had favoured her staying away, now that she was here he seemed to take a keen pleasure in her contribution. As she spoke he smiled affectionately at her, and looked at the others in the room to judge their reactions. The jurors gazed steadily at her. Even Miriam's mother spared her a few covert glances, pursed her lips knowingly, and nodded. They took it for granted that by now she was committed to Lord Stannard.

There was evidence of identification from the father and mother. Yes, that was their daughter, Miriam, and yes, she had been missing from home — and suddenly the father was pounding the back of a wooden chair in front of him, and yelling what he would do to the man who'd done this thing when he got his hands on him, and he wasn't going to rest until somebody paid, *somebody* . . .

Dr. Abbott shrilled, clutched at a strand of hair, and said that everybody present would sympathise with the feelings of the bereaved parents. There was a murmur of agreement. The mother pushed herself upright on the bench, and looked rather proud of her husband's outburst.

The Honourable Isabel Stannard testified that the deceased had been employed by her as lady's maid at Stannard Priory.

She had carried out her duties well until recently, when she had shown certain signs of flightiness.

'Flightiness, Miss Stannard?' the coroner encouraged her.

Isabel grimaced a cold apology at the parents. 'I'm afraid she had become somewhat impertinent. I felt she had other things on her mind.'

'But you did not dismiss her?'

'No. I had not yet reached a decision.'

'And when she left you without warning,' said Dr. Abbott deferentially, 'you were not as surprised as you might otherwise have been?'

'Not altogether.'

'You knew of no specific reason for this departure? She had never mentioned anything, or anybody, to you at any time?'

'Never.'

'Will you be kind enough to tell me exactly when she left your employ?'

Isabel, sometimes diffident at home, flinching from her brother's dominance and from her own private uncertainties, was cool and assured in this setting. She tossed answers disdainfully back: the

Wednesday evening when Miriam had last attended her, the Thursday morning when she was no longer there, the inquiries made of her cousin, one of the footmen, the message sent to her home, and the unhelpful reply.

'Nobody at home pursued the matter?' asked Dr. Abbott. 'Her departure was . . . accepted?'

'Not the first one round here,' muttered a disillusioned voice which proved to be that of the innkeeper, squeezing himself into a vacant space at the back of the room. This was his tavern, and he wanted to be part of the goings-on. The parish constable, standing behind the coroner, frowned a warning. But the grinning jurors appeared to find the comment eminently reasonable.

Dr. Abbott then presented his own medical report. The body whose discovery in the dried-up mere had been described by two witnesses and identified by both parents and employer as that of Miriam Fincham had met death by drowning. The stones deliberately attached to wrists and ankles made it clear that death had been criminally induced. No scrap of the deceased girl's clothing had yet been found, and there was nothing near the scene of death to indicate who might have been connected with the killing. If any person present had any relevant evidence to offer or, as an interested party, wished to raise any points, now was the time to put these before the court.

Sir Randall Gaunt spoke immediately. 'You say the girl was drowned.'

'It is sadly obvious.'

'You're sure she was not killed before being weighted and thrown into the mere?'

'There was no indication of strangulation, broken bones, or blows to the head. Apart from some peculiar incisions on the back — '

'Incisions?'

'Very deep scratches, shall we say.' Dr. Abbott tried to outstare his questioner. 'Deep enough to have drawn a considerable quantity of blood. I was unable to determine what instrument had been used to inflict these wounds, or with what purpose; but they would not in themselves have caused death.'

There was a whisper of horror around the room, which continued accusingly when Sir Randall spoke again.

'Were the lungs filled with water?'

Dr. Abbott became waspish. 'Are you questioning my medical competence, sir?'

'Were the lungs filled with water or were they not?'

'I find your attitude — '

'May I examine the body in your presence?'

'Certainly not.'

'Then call in an independent examiner. There must be a thorough autopsy.'

The word mumbled its way along the witnesses' bench and through the jurors. Miriam's mother let out a howl. 'Cut her up, you mean? That what you mean? As if it's not enough, her already marked the way she is, and now you want more of it. You!' she flung at Sir Randall.

Dr. Abbott said with some relish: 'No fear of that, Mrs. Fincham. Sir Randall is no longer qualified to practise.'

'I insist,' said Gaunt doggedly, 'on a proper autopsy.'

'Sir Randall, you are heard in this court as owner of the land on which the corpse was found. That interest does not allow you — '

'Interest, yes. Oh yes.' A young man pushed himself away from the wall near the witnesses' bench. 'On your land, yes. And happen you'd know what she was doing there? Happen you'd be able to explain them marks on her?'

'Alfred.' The coroner put his head back. 'If you have any questions to ask, they must be properly put through me.'

'And now you want to cut her up.'

The young man threw himself forward. He tripped over the sprawled feet of a juror at the end of the row, and smacked his full weight into Gaunt. The two of them thumped heavily against the wall. The young man's right fist began to lash out wildly. Gaunt took one blow against his left jaw and one into his shoulder, then forced himself upright and grabbed his assailant's arm.

Dr. Abbott hammered the table.

Deborah half-rose to her feet. Was nobody going to drag the frenzied young man away? The parish constable had turned to watch the fight, but made no move towards it. Justin's lips twitched with amusement.

It ended as quickly as it had begun. Some pressure of Sir Randall's fingers twisted the young man to one side, his arm at an unnatural angle. He groaned and doubled up.

Sir Randall said: 'I'll release you when you agree to carry on this discussion in civilised fashion.'

'Damn you.'

'Now then, sir.' The parish constable moved at last, towards Gaunt rather than the attacker.

Dr. Abbott said: 'I must insist on the dignity of this court being observed. Alfred, stand up and behave yourself.'

Warily, Gaunt released the young man.

'Now . . . ' said the coroner. He reached for his pen and dipped it in the brass inkwell. ' . . . if you have something to say, I am prepared to hear you. First, though, your full name.'

'You know my name, doctor. You just called me — '

'I have to observe official procedures.'

'Oh. Deeping, then. Alfred Deeping.'

The coroner scratched pen across paper and looked up. 'You wish to tell me something about the deceased?'

'I want to know what happened to her.'

'So do we all. Have you any assistance to offer?'

'Well, you know how it were with her and me.'

'Please tell the court.'

'Keeping company, weren't we? That wasn't no secret.'

'You were intending to marry?'

'That did seem so, but not right away. She was well suited where she was, and me only a ploughman. But I thought of getting a place t'other side of Thetford, maybe Honington way where it's better working than hereabouts, and then she might come round to it.'

'You were genuinely fond of Miriam?'

'Acourse I were.'

'There was no . . . quarrel between you?'

'Not what would lead to what you may be thinking.'

Justin raised an eyebrow and coughed gently, so that the coroner turned to glance at him. It was as if Justin were nudging his attention, prompting him.

Dr. Abbott said more severely: 'Alfred, will you swear that you did not attack Miriam Fincham?'

'That I did not.'

'But there *was* a quarrel?'

'Things wasn't faring too clever. She was starting to give herself airs, saying she knew places where she could do better than she'd ever do with me.'

'A young girl's teasing?'

'There were more to it than that. I couldn't think only that there was some other lad. But she went on about gentlemen friends, and how all of it was made worth her while.'

Awkwardly Mr. Fincham lumbered to his feet. 'Look, sir, that don't sound right to me, not letting him go on like that about our Miriam. If he's just trying to cover up something what he's done himself — '

'No!' cried young Deeping. 'I wouldn't kill her, never. You known me long enough, you know better'n that.'

Mrs. Fincham said: 'Sit you down, Jonas.'

Justin coughed discreetly again. 'I wonder if I might put a suggestion before the court?'

'By all means, m'lord.' Dr. Abbott was delighted.

'We all know it is no function of this inquiry to institute proceedings against any possible suspect. If, however, the verdict is one of murder, I will pledge the support of the Ingmere Association for rigorous investigation and the prosecution of anyone against whom a valid case is made.'

'But you don't believe that's me, sir ... my lord?' Young Deeping spread his arms despairingly. 'Mr. Fincham doesn't really, nor Mrs. Fincham. They *know* me.'

'But somebody did it,' said Justin. 'Or so the circumstances would seem to indicate.'

'Aye, somebody.' Deeping looked as though he might throw himself at Randall

Gaunt again. 'What about that girl, the one hanged herself a year or so back? Wanted her for dissection afterwards, didn't he, only they wouldn't let him nigh.'

'This is a gross slander,' said Gaunt quietly.

'And now what's to be done to Miriam? 'Gentleman friends'!' The young man spat it out.

'I need hardly say that I repudiate any such hysterical accusation. I would have thought it a function of the court to protect me from such. However, I would point out that the reference was in the plural, and I don't see myself as other than singular. Most singular, some people seem to think.'

The wry jest was above the heads of the jurors, who continued to study him with lowering suspicion.

'One final thing.' Gaunt's voice hardened. 'I would dispute the right of this court to accept or even to recommend at this stage the services of the Ingmere Prosecuting Society. It would surely be more fitting to think in terms of an impartial investigation carried out by trained men from the county police force or from London. That is the tendency of the law today.'

Dr. Abbott delivered his last thrust. 'I shall present my proper report and such recommendations as I think fit to the proper authorities, and I am confident they will see that justice is done.'

The verdict, agreed by the jury without a dissenting voice, was one of murder by a person or persons unknown.

★ ★ ★

Deborah and Isabel rose to leave. The men in the room, liberated from the gravity of the legal proceedings, were suddenly boisterous. They clattered to their feet, crowded back in jostling good humour to let the ladies pass, and roared out jokes about going through to the bar for a jug of ale, best suit or no best suit.

Justin had stopped for a word with the coroner. As he turned to join his sister and Deborah, there was the squeak of a trap opening through to another room.

Deborah caught a glimpse of Harry Chevening's face. Justin followed the innkeeper through an inner door. In the doorway he glanced back and indicated that he would be only a few minutes.

Deborah was glad to step out into the yard, needing the fresh air after the cramped, fetid room.

Isabel touched her arm. 'Let's not be in too much haste.'

Ahead of them, Sir Randall Gaunt was walking slowly, deep in thought, towards the heavy-beamed arch that led out from the stableyard. He remained unaware of two shapes waiting for him in the grey shadows until one of them scraped a boot on the cobbles. Then he looked up and stopped.

The two men edged towards him. One of them was Alfred Deeping, the other the dead girl's father. And beyond them, across the street, Deborah could see three or four others, waiting — perhaps ready to act, or simply there to watch.

'It would be better if we went back inside until Justin is ready,' said Isabel.

Deborah said: 'They will not dare . . . ?'

'Do let us go inside.'

Deborah stepped briskly out across the cobbles. The two men looked past Gaunt at her, and faltered. Sir Randall himself heard the click of her shoes on the stone and glanced back.

'Good morning, Sir Randall.'

He stared incredulously as she came up beside him and halted there.

She said: 'Will you walk me to the carriage? Lord Stannard appears to have been a trifle delayed.'

'Miss Ritchie.' It was the gentlest tone she had ever heard from him. 'If Lord Stannard is indoors, I think it better for you to wait there, within.'

'I'm sorry you find it distasteful to accompany me.'

Sir Randall said: 'I will not let you do this, Miss Ritchie.'

She slid his arm under hers with a smoothness she had learnt from accompanying and supporting her father so often. When she began to walk forward, he had to fall into step if they were not both to look absurd. Alfred Deeping

223

planted himself in their path.

'I beg you,' Gaunt murmured. 'Leave me. I can fend for myself.'

'And the herb garden, Sir Randall?' she said loudly and brightly. 'At this time of year it should be at its best.'

The rigidity of his arm slackened. She could feel laughter quivering through him. 'The damage you're doing! Now they will know I grow my own ingredients for wizards' potions!'

They both began to laugh, and walked straight at Alfred Deeping. His fists were clenched. He waited for Fincham to move into position beside him.

'Would you step aside a minute, miss?'

Deborah feigned surprise. 'I'm talking to this gentleman.'

'And I've got something I want to — '

'You best come with me, Alfred,' said Fincham.

Young Deeping, betrayed, stood his ground for a few seconds. Then, as Deborah and Sir Randall did not falter in their progress, he had to dodge to one side.

They came out into the street. The men

on the far side split up and sauntered away.

'I'm obliged to you, Miss Ritchie. Though I must say I'm unaccustomed to sheltering behind a lady's skirts.'

'You were always at least a footstep ahead of my hem, sir.'

It was ridiculous that they should both still be in such unpredictably happy, mercurial mood.

The Stannard carriage was drawn up opposite the main entrance to the inn. Sir Randall slowed as he led Deborah towards it. He was in no haste to let her go.

Their gaiety faded. 'It's said you are to marry Lord Stannard.'

'It has not been said by me.'

They stopped a few yards from the horses.

'And will not be said?'

'That's for Lord Stannard to ask rather than you, Sir Randall.'

'Not too late, then!' His good humour surged back, along with the echo of those words that had burst from him at Saxwold Hall. 'I said that when you had changed . . . knew you would change, *must* change . . . ' His hand moved towards hers, but they did not meet. He smiled. It was unnecessary for them to touch. 'We have so much to talk about, when you are ready.'

She could not fathom the cross-currents of her own emotions. At this stage they should be exchanging polite goodbyes. He would leave for Saxwold Hall while she waited for Isabel and Justin to rejoin her. Yet here they were, and she was in no greater hurry than Randall was for them to part. Curious eyes probably watched from behind the curtains. Still she felt light-hearted. The stranger beside her was ceasing to be a stranger. She was afraid to understand why, but given time — *When you are ready*, his words promised her — she would find out.

Let him not leave too soon. Let Justin not appear too soon.

'We seem to meet only on sad occasions.' He glanced ruefully at the inn. 'You'll associate me with inquests! And with my boorishness when we first met, and when I last tried to see you to your carriage. My haste to be done with the inquest upon your sister must have struck you as most unfeeling.'

'You wished to return to London. I understand that. And from my own point of view, there was nothing to be gained from dwelling on tragedy.'

'Unless one thereby avoided another tragedy.'

Memory struck a discordant note. The brooch, wrapped in tissue, rested in a drawer in her room at Stannard Priory. If she had been carrying it with her, she might have produced it and asked outright when he had last seen Beatrice wearing it. Instead she said: 'That poor girl we've just been hearing about. There's surely no possible connection with . . . what happened before.'

'Your sister,' he said. 'And that girl, and the other — the one who took her own life. And what else may there yet be to come?' Still he was not touching her hand but his whole being spoke urgently to her as if he had seized her. 'Leave with me now. To Saxwold Hall.'

'How could I possibly?' Then it struck her. 'You're not suggesting that *I* . . . ?'

'Deborah, please come with me.'

'It's unthinkable.'

He looked long and searchingly at her, and it had long ceased to be the dissecting, dehumanised gaze of a scientific recluse. The real man who had begun to emerge those few disconcerting days ago at Saxwold Hall was now in complete possession.

'I'll protect you,' he said. 'I swear it.'

'I'm not convinced I need protection.'

'And there's more. It's new to me, and I thought it would be hard to say after all these years. But I want to say it.' She waited, and he said simply: 'I need you. And I love you.'

Before she could frame any reply Justin and Isabel emerged from the inn. Justin's face set hard as he saw who was with Deborah.

Randall said: 'Please. Let it not be too late.'

'You know I can't possibly walk away . . . not now . . . couldn't accept such an invitation. Not until — '

'Until?'

'No, I don't know,' she said confusedly.

'When you are ready,' he said again tenderly. 'When you need me, I beg you not to delay. At any time, my dearest, I swear I'll not fail you.'

11

Justin said: 'I will not be made a laughing-stock.'

The wheels beneath them grated through a rut, the springs creaked, and they breasted the ridge.

'I saw nobody laughing.' Deborah remembered only that secret inner laughter she had shared with Randall Gaunt.

'They see you with me, and then see you associating with a man disgraced in his profession and mistrusted in his private affairs.'

'Mistrusted by whom?'

'I forbid you to consort with Gaunt.'

'Sir,' she reminded him, 'you do not yet have the right to choose whom I shall speak to and whom I shall not.'

Isabel huddled unhappily into a corner of the seat. Justin braced his legs against the swaying of the brougham, and leaned towards Deborah.

'For your own good, my dear, you must

be less wilful. You saw today how the folk of this neighbourhood feel about Gaunt. And it's a pity you didn't stay out of the way so that they might deal with him afterwards.'

'I thought of you as an upholder of the peace, not as one willing to turn a blind eye to violence.'

'Summary justice is all some men deserve.'

There was a silence. Deborah decided to let Justin simmer down.

At length Isabel said: 'I suppose it *was* that wretched young man who killed Miriam.'

'Our most likely quarry, yes,' Justin conceded.

'Yet you stood by,' said Deborah, 'while he wildly accused Sir Randall, and when he planned a physical assault on him. Why do you hate him so?'

'Let me say this and let it be the last we hear of it: Gaunt would do my family any harm that was at his disposal; he trifled with my sister's affections, he indulges in God knows what pastimes in that prison house of his, and he attempted to ensnare your half-sister. I do not want him near you.'

'I saw how he looked at you,' said Isabel. The hurt in her voice was stark and inescapable. Poor girl, thought Deborah, to be so hopelessly, helplessly in love with Randall Gaunt.

'And what his connection with this latest affair is,' said Justin, 'who's to tell?'

'You have just said you think the guilt is Alfred Deeping's.'

'We don't know what else there may be in it.'

Deborah said: 'At least Sir Randall is prepared to encourage an independent inquiry by qualified officers.'

'Qualified?' Justin snorted. 'Some new-fledged sergeant from a city investigation department, trying to find his way about the brecks? He'd be told only what they cared to tell, and find only what they wished him to.' He looked out over his passing territory. 'Animals are killed every day and night on the brecks: kill one another. And if some man or woman is killed, there's little difference. They're some of them little higher than animals.

But as cunning as animals in covering their tracks, and as ferocious when hunted down.'

'You mean it's too much trouble to seek the girl's murderer? Or too dangerous?'

'I'm saying that I and my colleagues know better what to do, and at what speed to do it.'

'You must always hold the power in your own hands, must you not?' she blazed. 'Nobody must set the pace or crack the whip but you.'

Justin laughed uproariously, rocking back in his seat. 'Splendid! I shall enjoy someone of your mettle.' He swished an imaginary whip. 'There'll be so much sport in the taming.'

Isabel laughed a protest, encouraging his exuberance. He was smiling at Deborah just as he had smiled so many times when he came in pursuit of her to Edinburgh.

She hoped he could not read what was in her mind, but it could not be kept there much longer. She must bring herself to tell him as soon as possible.

She knew that she was not going to marry Justin Stannard.

* * *

Waiting on the terrace as Justin came out and closed the casement door behind him, leaving his mother and Isabel to shrink tactfully into the background, Deborah was gripped by panic. Suddenly she was unsure that she could bring herself to say no. Once you had allowed a partner to lead you out on the floor, you did not abandon him halfway through a measure. From the start she had seen it as a dance, and enjoyed letting Justin guide her through its rhythms in the belief that she was still a free agent and might retreat when a lull came in the music. But if she rejected him now, it would be regarded as an outrageous breach of the proprieties. She saw herself trailing guiltily off on the long homeward journey.

So much easier to let herself be carried along. Nothing and nobody awaited her in Edinburgh.

But no: she would not be chatelaine of this mansion. She could never now be Lady Stannard.

Justin said: 'Too many things have come between us these past few days. I'll brook no interruptions this time.'

It was the consciousness of the terrace as a stage and of their having played part of this scene before that saved her. About to go through the prescribed words and gestures, she was overcome by a sense of the ridiculous. All she had to do was say one word, and the act would be finished, dying of its own absurdity.

'I will ask you again,' said Justin. He put out his hand and waited for her to take it in hers. 'Will you be my wife?'

It stuck in her throat; then was free. 'No. I'm sorry, but no, it's not possible.'

'Not possible?' He stared incredulously into her face and then at her hand, willing it to reach out and touch his.

'I'm so sorry, Justin. It's a very great honour, and I have been very troubled — '

'There's nothing that should trouble you. We shall make a good match of it, my dear . . . my dearest.' He seized her shoulders. 'I need you. This whole place needs you — but I most of all. You must not joke with me.'

'No. It is a serious matter, and I've given it the most serious thought. But you're wrong about it being a good match. That I know. Please do not ask me too much: it is difficult to explain, but I do know.'

His fingers tightened painfully. 'For how long have you been persuaded to think like this?'

'Justin, I have really tried to persuade myself to think the opposite. But in the end I've had to be honest and — '

'No!' His contorted face was blotting out the house, blotting out the entire sky. 'There's more to it. I can tell. In Edinburgh you were ready enough to consider marrying me. That I'd swear to. If I had asked you then — '

'It would have been most improper.'

'But if I *had* asked, you might have given way. It was certainly in your mind. It was in your mind when you travelled here with us, and has remained there since. You knew my intentions, you allowed me to suppose they would be well received. Even those few evenings ago, but for that accursed interruption I believe you would not have said no. So what has happened?'

'I've given the matter sober consideration,' said Deborah: 'that is what has happened. I should be sad if you thought I'd wantonly misled you.'

'Wantonly!' He pounced on the word. 'No, perhaps it's you who have been misled. That's it: you've been listening to Gaunt! What passed between you? What poison did he drip into your ear?'

'My decision is my own.'

'Gaunt up to his tricks.' Justin was beside himself. He began vengefully to shake her, to and fro, side to side. 'Deborah, you will marry me. You *must*. I will not let you go. My whole life . . . our life . . . I will not do without you. I will not.'

He pulled her suffocatingly close and kissed her. When she dragged her head away, he trapped it again, his mouth would not let hers go. It could have been a moment of ecstasy; but was distorted into one of fear and revulsion. Animals, Justin had called the breck folk. He was one of them now: an animal, ferocious in physical desire and in something more desperate and destructive.

Deborah let herself go limp. His hands slackened as she began to slide down, and she was able to straighten up abruptly and twist away from him. Gasping, she leaned against the balustrade and fingered her bruised lips. 'Please come no nearer.'

He stood panting. Then he shook his head, looked around him at grass and stone, tree and sky, and came back to reality. 'Forgive me.'

She said with a conciliatory smile: 'You are quick to anger if an answer displeases you.'

'What can I do to make things as they were?'

'They are as they always were.'

'Then we may start again?'

'I meant they should be left as they were.'

'If I am patient, and don't offend you again, and put my case more gracefully . . . ?'

'For both our sakes,' said Deborah, 'you must believe I have made the right decision.'

The storm threatened to mass and break out of him once more. Then, without a word, he spun on his heel and left her.

Shaken, Deborah went into the house. Heading slowly upstairs for her room, she passed a door on the first landing that so far had always been shut, but stood ajar.

'Deborah?'

Lady Stannard was sitting in a small armchair in the centre of a blue and white boudoir. She had her feet on a low footstool. It was a cosy little room, with a window looking down into the rose garden; but the placing of the chair and Lady Stannard's pose gave atmosphere of an audience chamber.

Deborah stood within the doorway, trying to gather her wits before this second confrontation.

'Well, my dear.' Lady Stannard smiled

expectantly. 'You have some news for me?'

'I think I must go home.'

'To make preparations?' said Lady Stannard archly. She glanced past Deborah. 'I do think Justin ought to have come to me first, or at the very least accompanied you.'

Deborah took a deep breath. 'I'm afraid there is nothing to prepare for, Lady Stannard. You have been most hospitable, but it's time for me to go back to Edinburgh.'

'For how long?' The older woman refused to take in what was being said to her.

'Edinburgh is my home. I have a lot to attend to there. I really must not neglect it any longer.'

The fine seams of Lady Stannard's face crinkled into dismay. Her little grimaces quickened like a muscular affliction. 'And this is all you have to say?'

'I'm sorry if you expected more of me.'

'But of course I expected more, girl. Has Justin . . . ' She clutched at a straw. 'Has he not yet spoken?'

'Your son has done me the honour of asking me to marry him. It is an honour I cannot accept.'

Lady Stannard pushed herself up from her chair and went to the window. She looked small and shrunken, ageing prematurely before Deborah's eyes. When at last she turned, she managed a defensive haughtiness. 'This is a great blow to me.'

'I am sorry.'

'I had been so sure you favoured him. From the first moment we met, I felt that all would go well.' She became more imperious. 'I must say that I see no reason why it should not.'

'It would be wrong for Lord Stannard's wife to be an uncertain, grudging one. He needs somebody very different.'

Lady Stannard moved her chair a fraction, and waved Deborah towards the padded blue ottoman in the window. 'Please sit down, my dear.' When Deborah was settled she went on: 'You're quite wrong. It is not somebody different he needs. It is you. He needs a *purpose*, and someone to give him the strength to follow that purpose and to guide him.'

'He is not a man to be easily led.'

'But you could do it. I think he realises this himself. And I believe that you, in your heart, you want to accept him.'

No reply was possible to such a wishful assertion.

'He needs you,' said Lady Stannard. 'You must be beside him. Save him from his follies — from that dissolute young Chevening, for one.'

'I would have thought that if Justin wished to be free, he could disengage himself by his own efforts.'

'He needs you,' Lady Stannard urged again. 'You can do it. I can think of nobody else who would. And you will see, Deborah, that it will be worth it, you'll be rewarded, I know how wonderful it can all be for you.'

Deborah in her turn edged round to look out of the window, wondering how best to make it clear, finally but with as little offence as possible, that her mind was made up.

Lady Stannard misinterpreted the movement. 'Perhaps Justin has rushed at it too boisterously. When he wants something, then he must have it at once. You will have to teach him many things, my dear.'

Deborah shook her head and got up. 'I think you'll want me to leave as soon as possible.'

'You cannot just hurry away at a moment's notice. Sleep on it. Please, for my sake, don't harden your mind against Justin simply out of pride. Think of accepting him. Think of it again. You will be deeply loved here at the priory. Think of the future you can make. The future *you* can make.'

★   ★   ★

The day after tomorrow, she would be gone. Deborah would gladly have left by the earliest possible train next morning, but the only one which made a suitable mainline connection for the north was very early indeed. Lady Stannard would not countenance such an unceremonious departure. If Deborah was set upon leaving, there was a ritual for this as for everything else. Another stroll in the gardens, some trivial talk of the weather and expressions of lasting affection and promises to meet again. In twenty-four hours — Deborah felt the undertow beneath every sentence — there was a chance she might change her mind and not go away at all. It was flattering that they should all three want her so much to stay; and unsettling.

Justin, morose, had ridden off somewhere late in the afternoon. Isabel had shied away from Deborah this past evening with that high-strung gaucheness which made her look arrogant to her inferiors, ill-assured to others. Justin dominated both her and their mother. When Justin had been crossed, they both shrank. Lady Stannard could just manage to put a good face on it. Isabel found it almost impossible to speak naturally.

'Do you realise what he'll be like when you have gone?' The laugh was poor camouflage for the accusation she stabbed at Deborah.

Think of accepting him. Think of it again.

If Deborah could still have been tempted, their sickly desperation would have warned her off. If Justin's salvation and their peace of mind depended so critically upon her, what kind of man must really lurk beneath the winning, boyish exterior he had endeavoured to present to her? *I will not let you go.* A greedy, spoilt little boy.

She lay calmly in bed, quite sure that she had done the right thing. After a while she got out of bed to open the window wider. She had grown used to the sound of the night here. Soon it would be a different night, different surroundings and sounds.

She propped her pillow against the bed-head, and sat half-upright. In the uppermost right-hand corner of the window lay the silver of a waning moon.

Justin had been quick enough to gallop away when she had rejected him; quick enough, she thought with a squirm of distaste, to seek easy solace elsewhere. Rounding up his cronies, no doubt, and roistering the night away. *Save him from his follies . . . you'll be rewarded . . .*

Inching herself up a fraction higher, she could just see the silvered claw above the priory ruins, and a faint shimmer of pale moonlight on leaves. Somewhere a door opened and closed. Justin slamming home, or a servant being summoned to refill a decanter or bring more bottles, would have been less disturbing than that faint, distant click and creak.

Deborah got out of bed. She reached the window in time to glimpse a dark shape vanishing into the trees. A woman's shape, she was positive. Then she was less positive. Moonlight created many a strange shape out of the branches. And beyond the branches — from the ruins shielded by the clump of trees came a brief, stabbing pinprick of light. A will-of-the-wisp, dancing over the moat like the lights she had been told of on Lantern Mere? But the meres and the priory moat were nearly bone dry.

She reached for the water carafe on the bedside table, and found it empty. Normally it would have been an irritation and no more. Tonight she was immediately convinced that she would not sleep unless she could have a glass of water. She tugged the bell pull to summon Kirstie. And the second it was done, she was ashamed of herself. It seemed Justin's impetuous, arrogant way of doing things was infectious!

She started towards the corridor to intercept Kirstie and tell her it was all right, and it didn't matter. The girl's room was at the far end of this landing, at the foot of a flight of stairs leading up to the lesser servants' bedrooms under the roof. Designed as a personal maid's quarters, it was connected to the guest bedroom in this wing by a bell wire. Deborah hesitated. It would do no harm for Kirstie to get up just once and bring her a fresh carafe. She ought to have checked that it was full.

There was silence. Kirstie did not appear. She must be a remarkably sound sleeper, unless perhaps the bell was not working. Deborah found herself walking along the corridor and the landing, up the three steps at the end, and into the recess off the staircase which led to the maid's room. She rapped lightly with her knuckles on the door.

'Kirstie?'

She turned the knob to open the door, and looked in. Little light filtered in past a buttress that half-obscured the window, but there was enough to show that the bed was empty.

It was not conscious decision, but something fatalistic that drove her back to her wardrobe. She dressed hurriedly and drew a cloak about her shoulders. A few minutes later she was letting herself out into the night.

She marvelled that she could be so foolhardy. What was she expecting to find? She was scared but curious: not as scared as she might have been when she first came here, such a short time ago, for she had already come to sense the moods of the countryside under sun or moon or wind.

When she skirted the trees and came out above the parched moat, the priory ruins made a silver silhouette. They looked insubstantial, wraithlike. No sound came from them. Deborah stood on the edge of the moat, listening to that detached half of herself telling her to go back to bed and stop behaving so outrageously.

There were voices! She heard them without really hearing. A murmur, the cadence of a higher voice, and spasmodic laughter. Was it imagination? It was eerie and damped down, not loud enough to be real. The ghosts of ancient monks, intoning their rites, could make such ethereal sounds as they processed in and out of the remnants of their mutilated chapel. Lady Stannard had been right: it was enough to drive any superstitious intruder hastily away from the Stannard estate.

Deborah lowered herself cautiously into the moat, testing the solidity of its bed. There was a damp patch in the middle, and at one point a squelch of mud which nearly snatched the shoe from her foot, but she reached the inner bank and the island without trouble.

She wished that at some stage she had persuaded one of the family to escort her to the ruins so that she would know their hazards. Light and shadow were deceptive. The gaping mouth of a doorway might lead to a dangerous fall. But as she warily approached it, the voices grew stronger.

One part of the fabric seemed almost intact. There was no glass in the windows, but the roof was still on and when she entered, a cautious step at a time, she came up against some solid construction in the middle of the chamber. Her hand traced out a filigree of stone screen. As her eyes grew accustomed to the different textures of the gloom, she could just make out the shape of an ornamented tomb. She guided herself warily round it.

There was a pale but distinct line of light across the floor beside the tomb. The erosion of centuries, or perhaps the impact of some slab of falling masonry, had cracked two flagstones. The light came from what must be a vault beneath the floor of the chantry. But how did one get into it?

Deborah followed the crack across the floor until it died out against a creeper-shrouded wall. A few feet away was a circular turret staircase, spiralling both up and down. The light from below was still shaded and diffused, but when she descended three steps it grew brighter. She squeezed her way down, one hand against the rough cold wall, until she reached a flat space at the bottom.

Another tomb was set across the exit from the stairwell. An alabaster man and woman lay on their backs, hands clasped together, staring sightlessly up at the white tracery of the canopy. Through the lacy stonework Deborah saw, past the two dead profiles, two living faces lit by a glowing brazier. They were the flushed, inflamed faces of Harry Chevening and Justin Stannard.

The backs of two other heads moved round to block them from her view. Then there was a jostling of two more, and a girl squealed a protest and then giggled; and Kirstie Hamilton's tousled head and bare shoulders bobbed up for a moment and then plunged down again. Deborah advanced to the edge of the tomb. She could not credit what she saw, but could not turn away and make her escape.

One man with his back to her was

prodding and slapping Kirstie with abstracted playfulness, but his attention was not on her. He and the other men were on their knees about a small hollow in the ground. At first Deborah could not make out what was happening, then she heard a raucous squawk and a wild flurry of wings. Chevening breathed a feverish oath. There was a mad flutter, a breathless pause, and then one man saying, 'Throw the damn thing back in,' and another screech and scatter of dust, and a couple of feathers drifting up and drifting away.

It was a cock-fight. In the infernal glow of the brazier, Deborah saw sweat on Justin's brow, and his lips praying or cursing. With him, there was little distinction.

Then the picture was obscured as Kirstie stood groggily upright, holding a tankard from which she was trying to drink. Wine spilled over her shoulder. She reeled back against the tomb, so close that Deborah could have reached out and touched her. She seemed, in the red and black nightmare of lurching shadows, to be wearing little more than a rough leather kirtle, exposing her plump arms and the fullness of her thighs.

Chevening let out a yell of triumph. The men crouched forward. There was a gloating murmur, and Chevening made a downward thrust as if to ensure a death blow.

They all sat back, sated.

Only Justin, still scarlet from the heat of the fire and the contest, was petrified where he knelt. He might himself have been a doomed cock with no more strength for the fight.

'Let me see,' said Chevening. 'Almost five thousand now, I fancy.'

One of the other men got to his feet and made a playful grab at Kirstie. She dodged away. He grabbed something from a hook on the wall, and as he brandished it there came the crack of a whip. Kirstie squealed, half-frightened and half-tempting. The whip cracked again. She ducked and ran round the tomb, blundering straight into Deborah.

Kirstie screamed again.

Hard on her heels, her pursuer came to

a halt. Peering at Deborah in the web of shadow, he let out a moan more agonised than Kirstie's cry.

'It's her! She's come back!'

Harry Chevening snatched a torch from an iron bracket and held it high above his head. He staggered towards the tomb and thrust the light across the upturned faces of the dead lord and his lady.

'Well! Upon my soul.' He began to wave the torch to and fro, so that smoke bit at Deborah's eyes and nose. 'Justin, look who's come to join the revels.'

12

In the shallow pit lay the dead cock, its defeated spurs bloody in the torchlight. Beyond it, at the end of the vault, two black candles burned on a stone altar. Justin stormed across the floor, intoxicated by wine and some other more dangerous fantasy.

The young man who had been pursuing Kirstie mopped his brow. 'I thought ... that face, I'd have sworn ... her, come back to — '

Justin knocked him aside and brushed past Chevening. Arms akimbo, he confronted Deborah. 'What the devil are you doing here?'

'You, rather than I, appear to be interested in the devil's work.' She was icy cold and not afraid of him or of anything in this place. Its trappings were disturbing, but she sensed their emptiness. Torches in brackets along the walls cast a fiendish glow, strengthened in the middle of the vault by the coals of the brazier. A flagon of wine, fallen on its side, spilled a dark red trickle down the altar steps. One man slumped against a bench and tried in vain to lift a silver goblet to his lips. Kirstie fumbled back to reality through her stupor, clutching the leather kirtle to her. Her legs were bare to the knee, and there was a greasy line across her perspiring neck.

Deborah had read of the Hell-Fire Club and the blasphemous, sham monks of Medmenham, and of other such associations. There had been strange cults in Transylvania and in some of the dark forests not far from the watering-places where her father had sought cures. But here below Stannard Priory ruins, she surveyed with all the scorn and certainty of her good kirk upbringing a shoddy travesty, the tawdry nonsense of bored young ne'er-do-wells playing at evil.

'Are you pleased?' Justin roared. 'Pleased with where your spying has led you?'

He was clad entirely in black silk. He might have been splendid and fearsome.

Deborah found him absurd. She said: 'Kirstie, you will return with me to the house. We leave in the morning. I owe this family no further courtesies.'

'This will never do,' said Chevening.

Justin let out a snarl of frustration. 'All right, be off home with you, the whole pack of you. The meeting's ended.'

'Calling a halt now?' said Chevening. 'When the whole thing is becoming so interesting? I had supposed the future Lady Stannard was preparing to share *all* her husband's diversions.'

Deborah looked her loathing at him. How alike he and Justin were, inseparable as twins or as opposite sides of a coin: Justin light, Chevening dark. But the dark had encroached too far upon the light.

'I will accompany you back to the house,' said Justin.

'There's no need. I'll fare better on my own with this girl you've so despicably — '

'I will accompany you.' Justin staggered, and steadied himself. 'The rest of you — be off.'

Chevening said in an insinuatingly

polite tone: 'Leave the matter to me. I'll see that the premises are tidied and locked up before I go. Goodnight to you, ma'am . . . miss . . . my lord.'

Justin took Deborah's arm. She shook him off and indicated that Kirstie should precede her up the stairwell.

'Miss Deborah, I can't see. And I'm no feeling well.'

Chevening came forward with a flourish and handed her a storm lantern. Dismally Kirstie stumbled up the steps. Deborah followed. After a muttered exchange with Chevening, Justin came up behind her.

Kirstie nearly dropped the lantern as she stumbled across the moat. It wavered an erratic path over the grass.

Justin caught up with Deborah. 'It was the last time, I swear it. It was folly. But I was distraught; your rejection had come as a bitter shock. I allowed myself to slip too easily back into . . . into old stupidities.'

'And to drag my maid with you. How many others have you treated in this fashion? Did they include Miriam? And that girl who hanged herself?'

Kirstie moaned and dropped the lantern. They heard her retch hideously. As Justin groped for the lantern, she was sick, over and over again until there was nothing left but whining breath. They had to half-carry her back to her room.

Justin said: 'You cannot leave first thing in the morning with the girl in that state.'

'You'll use any excuse to keep me, sir.'

'I will indeed.' Even now the spark of hope was not extinguished.

But he was right. Put to bed, Kirstie was a ghastly sight. Deborah washed her and supported her each time she sagged; and then realised the girl's own clothes must be still somewhere in the ruins. Kirstie, so far from attending on her during the journey, was clearly unfit to travel; and Deborah was tired, with a sickness of heart and soul which was quite different from Kirstie's.

There was a whimper from the bed. 'What ha' ye in mind for me, Miss Deborah?'

'I'll see you safely home to Edinburgh, which is more than you deserve.'

'Oh, Miss Deborah — oh, what'll Mr. MacKenzie be saying about it all?'

'You'll find out, that I'll be bound.'

Deborah left Kirstie to her woes before she began to feel too sorry for the girl.

★ ★ ★

There was no sign of Justin during the course of the morning. Lady Stannard was at her most effusive, until Deborah's inability to make more than the most clipped response at last dawned on her.

'Is there something wrong, my dear?'

Deborah had no intention of revealing Justin's shabby secrets to his mother — if they were secrets. She suspected that Lady Stannard must all along have known something of what went on in the ruins. She was tempted to suggest that she spend this next night at the inn by the station. But Deborah shrank from hurting this unsettled, perplexed woman any further.

Late in the morning, Deborah went to check on Kirstie. Her face was a sickly yellow. She struggled to get out of bed, but Deborah forced her gently back.

'You'd best stay where you are for a while. I'll have one of the maids bring you some food.'

'Och, miss, I'm not fancying anything to eat.'

'You'll have hot broth,' said Deborah. 'I'll tell them you've had an upset stomach.'

On her way along the landing, she looked out of the window on the turn of the stair. A flicker of unusual colour moved on the ridge beyond the northern wall of the park. It was a gypsy caravan. If it continued on that route, it would have to turn down the lane towards the entrance gates.

There was a sudden clatter of hoofs below. Justin came from under the lee of the house, riding towards the drive, hunched forward. She could not see his face but guessed its expression: he, too, had seen or been told of the caravan, and was racing off to wreck his spite on the presumptuous traveller who dared come this close.

He disappeared into the lime avenue.

The caravan dipped down from the ridge. Deborah could almost feel the impact of their impending collision.

Justin didn't appear for lunch. Either he was indulging in an extended persecution of the gypsy or he was deliberately avoiding Deborah. The meal was eaten largely in silence. Lady Stannard, having accepted that further attempts to sway her would be fruitless, was sulking. Isabel asked Deborah a few desultory questions, and then let the conversation lapse.

In the afternoon Deborah sat at her dressing-table, emptying the drawers in readiness for packing her cases. She took Beatrice's brooch from its tissue and contemplated it yet again. It still told her nothing.

There was a tap at the door. Isabel came in. 'Would you like me to send Emmeline in to help you? I hear your maid's not well.'

'She was out late,' said Deborah.

'I wouldn't have thought there was much entertainment for a girl of her kind in this neighbourhood.'

'I think you know about Justin's little

amusements,' Deborah accused.

'I know that sometimes he . . . that he and Chevening and some others tend to become somewhat wild. But I've never asked where they go, or what they do.'

'I went last night to find out.'

'Deborah, you don't mean . . . they weren't . . . not Kirstie?'

'That is what I mean.'

Isabel drooped wretchedly beside the dressing-table. 'He was very upset by your refusal to marry him. I suppose he sought some kind of forgetfulness.'

'You make it sound that I am to blame!' exploded Deborah.

'No, of course not. It was just that we did hope, for his sake . . . ' Isabel looked down, seemed to droop further, and gasped. 'Wherever did you find my brooch?'

Deborah picked up the little twist of gold and garnets. 'This is — *your* brooch?'

'Beatrice gave it to me a few months ago. I believe it had been a present. I'd thought it most attractive, and commented on it. She said I could have it for all she cared; it wasn't at all her style.'

'I found it at Saxwold Hall.'

Isabel coloured. 'I wondered, when I realised I had lost it, if that was where it could be.'

'You didn't ask?'

'No. I wasn't at all sure, and by then I . . . we were not . . . I did not care to trouble Sir Randall.' She put a hand on Deborah's shoulder and slid down beside her on the stool. 'Deborah, I wish you would stay, and we could be sisters. But I don't blame you for wishing to be done with us. Justin isn't worthy of you, though Mama thinks you could make him so. But there could be such heartbreak . . . ' Their two faces were side by side in the glass. Isabel found it easier to talk to the reflections. 'He would have used you,' she said, 'as he tries to use everybody. And when things went wrong, he would turn on you. I'm his sister, and I know this. He wanted me to marry Randall Gaunt — '

'But I thought they were mortal enemies.'

'Since Justin was thwarted, yes. When he had the notion of the two estates being joined, and of getting his hands on some of Randall's money — they were friends.'

'Money? But surely — '

'You have seen what he's like when the gambling fever is on him. Sometimes he wins — '

'Edwin!' cried Deborah. '*That* is where Edwin's money went. And after it, Beatrice's.'

'I . . . I imagine so. But when he has won, he cannot keep it. Looking back, I know he must have suffered some heavy loss just before he threw me at Randall's head.'

'Was it so painful?'

'I became . . . very fond of him. Justin's plans soon ceased to concern me. I hoped that for my own sake it would all come right. But Randall was still lost in the past. I thought he was beginning to care for me.' All at once it came rushing out of her. 'He liked me, he was attentive and most agreeable — but he hadn't realised how deeply attached to him I'd become. When he awoke to the situation, he was most . . . considerate.' Her voice became bitter. 'He did all he could to ensure that

I did not feel humiliated. But courtesy and consideration were not what I wanted from him.'

'And not what you got from Justin, I imagine.'

'Randall never trusted my brother. Word of Justin's escapades must have reached his ears, and he would know the company Justin keeps. But his disapproval was as nothing compared with Justin's anger. Once it was clear there was to be no union of Stannard and Gaunt, Justin turned utterly against him. He reviled him, lost no opportunity of speaking against him in public or private.'

'But you went on seeing Sir Randall?'

'We met occasionally. And then once, when Justin was away, he asked me to a dinner party at Saxwold Hall. I fancy he thought he was making it easier for me — trying to establish some sort of undemanding friendship. I was too upset to make any kind of showing. I was scared of what Justin would say if he found out, scared of myself; and I suppose that was when I lost the brooch, and did not even think of it again until much later.'

Deborah said: 'Once or twice you have hinted that Sir Randall's interests lay with Beatrice.'

'It is something I've told myself to explain why he would not have me. And I know it to be untrue . . . and contemptible.' Isabel began to get up. 'I should not have told you all this.'

Impulsively, Deborah caught her hand and pressed it. 'I'm glad you did. And I, too, am sorry we shall not be sisters.'

'Perhaps it's as well you're going. I saw,' she recollected, 'how Randall looked at you when . . . There, you see — jealousy again, telling myself lies to comfort myself. Please pretend it was never said.'

As Isabel reached the door, Deborah said: 'Since I shall never marry Justin, tell me now: it was only my money he wanted, was it not?'

'He loved you,' said Isabel. 'The money, yes. But also he loved you. And since you have spurned him, he'll hate you.'

*　*　*

Some ten minutes after Isabel had left, Deborah heard footsteps pass her door. They went in the direction of the servants' staircase at the end of the corridor, then stopped. She thought of Kirstie, and wondered how the girl was getting along.

As she went towards the maid's room, the door opened and Justin came out. Incensed, Deborah quickened her pace. 'Please keep away from the girl! Haven't you done her enough mischief?'

His face was ashen and he walked like a man in a trance. The aftermath of his night of debauchery? He looked far more cowed and stricken than Kirstie.

'I have returned the clothes she left in the vault,' he said dully. Light from the window picked out a moistness in his eyes. He stared wonderingly at Deborah, then walked past her.

At dinner, Lady Stannard berated him. Where had he been all day? Taking his disappointments like a spoilt child was too degrading. She talked on, and when Isabel turned to Deborah affectionately and tried to start a more comfortable conversation, her mother talked her down.

Justin stared again at Deborah with a mixture of puzzlement and something sly, the beginnings of some furtive calculation. She excused herself as soon as it was reasonable to do so, saying that she had packing to complete and would like to retire early.

'And may I be sure of being wakened in good time for the morning train?'

'I shall drive you to the station myself,' said Justin in an oddly flat voice. As she left the room, he suddenly rose and caught up with her in the hall. 'You will never forgive me for the foolishness of last night.' He made it an accusation rather than a plea.

'I want only to leave here,' said Deborah.

'You'll not listen to me? If I swear it was a last stupidity, never to be repeated?'

'I think you will always find it difficult to resist the blandishments of your friends.'

'You could help me.'

Deborah was at the end of her tether.

'Lord Stannard, I have spent some years looking after a gallant man crippled in the service of his Queen. I didn't begrudge one moment of it. Am I now to spend the rest of my life as custodian of a libertine without the strength or dignity to curb his perverse appetites?'

Justin turned and walked in that same trance-like way back into the room.

Upstairs, Deborah summoned Kirstie, who was still pale but able to help with folding dresses and packing the trunk for them both. When they had finished, Deborah said: 'I'd like some hot water in half an hour.'

'Very good, miss.'

Deborah tidied up a few final items, and wound her travelling clock, propped open on the bedside table. When Kirstie returned with the large jug of hot water, she was also carrying a mug from which a little spiral of steam rose aromatically.

'I thought, Miss Deborah, you might like a warm drink. They make it every night for her ladyship, and I thought perhaps you'd be liking a wee taste instead of just hot water.' It was a clumsy attempt to ingratiate herself. Deborah smiled and took the mug, inhaled, and took a sip. It was hot honey and lemon, over-sweet but soothing.

'Thank you, Kirstie.'

The girl curtsied and backed away. She looked frightened, as if she had all along expected Deborah to reject the peace offering.

Deborah put the mug down and went to the window. It was the last time she would look out on the night and on the grounds. The wind was getting up, and the branches of the trees began to moan and fidget against the sky. There was a movement of something or somebody against the extreme edge of the clump.

Deborah watched. It could have been a swaying branch. Then, she was sure, there came a spark of light from the direction of the ruins. So much for Justin's promises of reform! Doubtless he was excusing himself by saying that if she was so hard-hearted, he was entitled to disport himself with others as he chose. Abruptly she had a picture of him emerging from Kirstie's room after returning her clothes.

She hurried along to make sure that the girl was still there.

Kirstie sat up in bed, startled, looking more fearful than ever. Deborah studied her for a moment, then turned to the door. Inside there was a key in the lock. She took it out. 'What's that you're doing, miss?'

'I propose to lock you in. I think I owe it to you, and to Mr. MacKenzie, to make absolutely sure.'

'But if the house was to catch fire, and I couldnae get out, or — '

'I can't imagine why the house should catch fire. If it does, I'll come to your rescue at once.'

Deborah went out, and, feeling inordinately prim and self-conscious, turned the key in the lock and took it away with her. When she saw the drink by her bedside, she nearly relented. By the time she got into bed, the concoction was lukewarm. The cloying aftertaste was more noticeable than when it had been hot. Still she was glad of it. She emptied the mug and put it down beside the clock.

Isabel's confession and the memory of

last night blurred into one certainty. It was unthinkable that Beatrice should take part in Justin Stannard's lecheries. Yet somehow the trail to Beatrice led not through Saxwold Hall but through here. Too late now to follow it, for she was leaving in so few hours from now. Too late, now, to go after Beatrice.

Going after Beatrice . . .

Beatrice was performing a drunken dance. Deborah tried to reach out and stop her, but Beatrice fled away down a long stone corridor to an altar which proved to be a huge candle. The flames were dark and smoky. Deborah turned away from the swirling darkness to see Edwin — faceless, for she had never known his face — throwing dice onto a pack of cards and then flailing the cards with a dead cockerel held by one leg. She wanted to tell him that the flap of his pocket was open and that money was pouring out on to the stone floor, but when she opened her mouth no sound would come out. Beatrice had to be told, before all her money was lost, too. Deborah set off in pursuit again, with

Beatrice forever running ahead and ignoring calls to stop and explain.

They were slowly getting closer to the altar. The flames of the candles began to burn brighter and brighter, hurting Deborah's eyes. She turned her head, and felt the softness of the pillow under her ear. The sun was streaming in through the window. She rolled over to look at her clock, on the table beside the empty mug.

It was past nine o'clock. She had missed her train.

13

'But Miss Deborah,' Kirstie protested, 'wasnae it you what locked me in? I woke up in good time, but I couldnae get out of my room.'

'If you'd knocked, or called, somebody must have heard.'

'That they did not. I knocked and I shouted, but me being all that way from the servants' quarters, and them from upstairs being up and about in other parts of the house, I suppose, there'd be none to hear.'

Deborah went back to her room and hurriedly completed her toilet, then went downstairs in a rare mood for battle.

There was nobody about. Deborah was at a loss. The inhabitants could not all have been spirited away; but they were being very reticent this morning.

In the breakfast room places were laid, and there was a breath of warmth from the chafing-dishes on the sideboard.

Deborah rang. After an age, a footman appeared.

'Good morning, miss.'

'Were no instructions given that I was to be woken early and that the carriage would be taking me to the station?'

'Not to me, miss. Shall I enquire while you take breakfast?'

'Is Lady Stannard not down? Or Lord Stannard?'

'Apparently not, miss.'

Deborah looked angrily at the table. Obviously she must eat something, with a long and now complicated journey ahead.

'You'll see that someone is ready to take me to Ingmere?'

'I'm sure his lordship will arrange it, miss.'

The man withdrew, leaving her with only the sound of the wind for company until Justin came into the room. She had been trying to make herself eat a slice of ham. Now she pushed her chair back and stood up indignantly.

'What sort of treatment is this, sir? A promise that I should be away in good time this morning, and — '

'It seems we all overslept.' He was haggard, his eyes red-rimmed; but there was a sly gleam in them. 'I fear I sat up too late.'

'Finding entertainment in your priory, no doubt.'

'No, madam; I was revising my plans for the future. Doing some calculation.'

'But could the carriage not have been ready for me? I need not have disturbed you. All I wish is to be gone. Yet there is no arrangement, there is nobody about, your mother and Isabel — '

'I can explain that. I asked them to keep to their rooms this morning, as I wished to be alone with you on the journey to the station. They understood my feelings.'

'And the servants?' said Deborah. 'The coachman who ought to have been waiting — can you explain that?'

'I own it's my fault. In the middle of my other concerns, I omitted to give the proper orders. I was relying on being up early myself and setting things in train then. But I failed.'

'I should be grateful if you would now

do whatever's necessary for my departure.'

'There is no other train of any use to you today.'

'I'm prepared to make myself comfortable at the inn until there *is* a train. Even if I can get only so far as York or some such place, I'll gladly spend this next night there.'

Justin helped himself to kidneys from a silver dish. 'I accept that you have rejected me. Must you now treat me as an enemy?'

'I'm sorry. But why,' cried Deborah, 'should you wish to keep me here?'

'Why, indeed? You make it clear that you entertain no thought of changing your decision. What purpose could I possibly have in holding you here against your will?'

The slyness of his manner took away from the innocent reassurance of his words. 'I shan't inconvenience you or your staff any further. If I might hire a vehicle — '

'From where?' He stood looking out of the window, holding his plate. Past his brooding profile, she saw the dust cloud shimmering along the horizon. 'It's thickening badly across the breck. No Ingmere driver would venture out in such conditions.'

'So I'm a prisoner.'

'Better that, for a while, than being trapped because of setting out as we'd originally intended.'

'I doubt that you ever had any such intention.' The room, his presence, the entire building and its family weighed down on her. Fear cracked like a whip across her mind. She said: 'What did you do to Beatrice?'

'I?'

'You were the man in that letter of hers. You were the one, I know it, the one who drove her to . . . to . . . ' Words would not come because she still did not know what Beatrice's ultimate terror had been. 'And the others,' she said.

Without answering, he moved away from the window and quietly set down his empty plate on a marble shelf.

'The others,' she repeated. 'That girl in the mere — how did she die? From the pain of what you inflicted on her in that foul cellar?' A muscle under his left eye twitched. 'And the suicide,' said Deborah. 'Was her shame so great?'

'I'll not have you spreading such slanders throughout the country,' he said.

'I assure you that when I leave here, my only wish — '

'You will not leave here,' he said, 'until I have your promise that you'll curb your tongue.'

'You can't keep me here forever. And if I'm silent, it's because I choose to be so. Before I make any promise, you must tell me the truth. All of it.'

He crossed the room to the door. 'I'll send Draper out to assess the drift later in the morning,' he said remotely, as if it had no bearing on anything they had just been saying.

Deborah went shakily out on to the terrace; then came back in again, summoned the crestfallen Kirstie and ordered her to be ready at a moment's notice in case the wind should change or Justin should come back with some perfectly normal suggestion or some unpredictable opportunity should present itself. Still there was no sign of Lady Stannard. Kirstie reported that she was confined to her room with a headache.

Isabel came down at last, complaining that she too had a headache. And she had overslept. It was true that Justin had asked her and her mother to let him accompany Deborah to the station on his own. 'I told you, he loved you. However distressed he may be now, he still wished to play out his last romantic little scene. Mother and I were to say goodbye, though. I can't think how — '

'Did you take a warming drink last night at bedtime?'

'My mother always has one. Last night my maid brought me one also.'

'And you drank it?'

'One does in such circumstances, doesn't one?'

Deborah went off to Kirstie's room. She closed the door and stood over the maid.

Kirstie cowered back.

'Who ordered you to bring me that drink last night?'

'Ordered, miss? I thought you'd be glad of it, I was just there and I thought — '

'Somebody told you, and told Miss Stannard's maid, to bring us those drinks. And what were you told to put in them?'

Kirstie shook with fright. 'Miss Deborah, it was just a wee drink I thought you'd like, and maybe it was that Emmeline heard me and thought it would be a fine idea for Miss Isabel as well.'

She was so terror-stricken at this revival of Deborah's sternness towards her that Deborah could not bring herself to pursue the matter. But when she went away she was not satisfied.

On impulse she went up to the first landing door behind which lay Lady Stannard's boudoir. She tapped, waited, opened the door; but the bright little room was empty.

The entire house felt empty. The servants, always unobtrusive, had withdrawn altogether into some eerie, hidden world she could not hope to penetrate. Halfway along one corridor she was sure had run the full uninterrupted length of the house last time she had walked along it, there was a locked door.

Turning back, she could have sworn there was a movement of somebody dodging back into a side passage. It was ridiculous to be so sure that the unseen person, if there had ever been one at all, was Justin. She must not let the place or this exasperating, protracted wait demoralise her. She went out towards the gardens.

The wind struck at her. Although there was no visible rush of sand across the parkland, she could feel the faint sting of tiny particles against her skin. At the west end of the house a sudden eddy buffeted her, and round the corner she moved closer in to the shelter of the wall. Above were the shuttered windows. If Justin had married her, and if she had restrained him from gambling her fortune away, would he have opened up the rooms and corridors at this end and filled them with life again?

She glanced up at the turrets, striking eccentric angles against the sky. A badly eroded cornice seemed to sway in the wind.

Suddenly she knew it was no illusion. A large white slab of masonry was rocking, tilting out too far.

Deborah threw herself towards the steps, leading down into the sunken garden. Behind her there was a crash which shook the ground. A flying chip of stone grazed her wrist, and she wrenched her ankle as she fell down two steps. After an uncountable number of seconds she pushed herself up into a sitting position and looked back. Jagged fragments lay in a scatter of white and grey about the spot where she had been standing only those seconds ago.

Her ankle was painful, but it bore her weight. Slowly she hobbled back into the house, making her way to the foot of the servants' staircase. The door there was bolted from the other side. In itself that was suspicious. It meant that by the time she found another way to the top, whoever had been up there would have got away. Because someone had been there, of that she was sure.

There was no sound from the kitchens, no sign of anyone in the corridors. She found herself a comfortable chair and waited, furious and afraid, for Justin to reappear.

The house was so still within itself that Deborah heard Isabel the moment she began to cross the hall. The footsteps came close to the open door, which Deborah was facing just as Lady Stannard had faced her boudoir door, commanding a view of anyone who passed.

Isabel stopped and stared in. 'Is something wrong? You look so ... so strange.'

Deborah told her, brusquely and concisely, what had happened. Isabel came slowly into the room, shaking her head in disbelief.

'I find it too strange a coincidence,' Deborah concluded, 'that the stone should have fallen at just that moment, on to the very spot where I had been standing.'

'But you can't suppose it was deliberate?'

'You told me that your brother would hate me now.'

'Enough to murder you? Deborah, this is madness. I will not listen to such dreadful talk. To kill you? To what end?'

Deborah had no answer. Of course such a killing would have been purposeless. Nevertheless she sat rigid, still on the alert for she knew not what. Reluctantly, she said: 'You must bear with me. It was very upsetting. I don't know how it came about. Don't know what I'm saying.'

Justin returned late for lunch, explaining that several estate problems had arisen all at once. It seemed to Deborah that he was announcing it more loudly than was necessary. 'Draper has news from the warreners,' he boomed as he sat down, adding for Deborah's benefit: 'They have this telegraph system of their own, you know. Amazing how swiftly word can run from one side of the breck to the other. News takes little longer than it would by express mail.'

'News?' Isabel prompted.

'The railway line is blocked. It'll take a good team to clear it when the wind drops. We may hire out some of our labourers, as they're here on the scene.'

'That's where you've been most of the morning?' said Isabel with a meaningful glance at Deborah.

He followed her glance, and Deborah was afraid again.

'You don't look yourself.'

'Deborah has had a severe shock.'

She had to explain. It came out as little more than a confused account of some childish accident.

Justin got up. 'This is appalling!' How good an actor was he; how much sheer enjoyment was there in his outrage, his decisive stride towards the door?

When he returned, he was shaking his head. 'Something will have to be done about that end of the building. We have put off renovations too long.' He came round the table to Deborah and leaned solicitously over her. 'This is not what I would have wished at all. I'm deeply shaken by it. But since you cannot leave in any case, please rest; please ask for whatever you want.'

I want, she said so clearly in her mind that she was surprised they did not hear her, *to go away. I want a carriage at the door within five minutes. Please.*

'Yes, you must rest,' said Lady Stannard peevishly. She had been listening to the tale of mishaps without appearing to take much in. Her attitude towards Deborah was not one of apology for the inconveniences suffered, nor horror at the near accident. Deborah had chosen not to be one of them. It was high time she left.

In this, thought Deborah, they were in agreement. Before the meal was over, she knew that she must get away, whatever the cost. Remembering what Justin had said of the warreners, she wondered if a message could be sent to Ingmere on her behalf; or to Saxwold Hall. But it was hardly worth considering. Any such message would somehow turn back on itself and reach Justin's ears first.

She must walk out or ride out alone, unencumbered by cases or any other personal belongings save what she wore. Randall Gaunt had begged her to seek him out when she needed him. Now, assuredly, she needed him. This house was closing in on her. Justin, saying one thing and meaning something quite different — something she could not fathom — was playing some wicked game with her. She could not wait for its outcome.

The wind was driving hard along the ridge, but she could not believe that in broad daylight the roads would be impassable. She knew general directions to and from Stannard Priory well enough. She could find her way to Saxwold Hall.

'You must rest.' It was an order, delivered before he went off to issue, presumably, other orders to those invisible servants and estate workers. 'Isabel, I rely on you to make Deborah rest.'

It took a full twenty minutes to get rid of Isabel. Deborah had to endure being settled beside one of the terrace windows with her ankle on a footstool, and an occasional table with a handbell close to her arm. Kirstie was sent in with a number of books and magazines, which she pushed timorously closer along the table, as if afraid of a stroke across the knuckles. Isabel fussed to and fro, equally nervous — scared of her brother, and scared of what Deborah might say about him.

At last she went off to her room, promising to come back shortly to see if Deborah needed anything further. How incredible it was that she should ever have contemplated entering this household as a bride, as the new mistress of Stannard Priory!

With Isabel gone, sound and breath were again sucked slowly out of the room. Everyone retreated, backing away from her, leaving her until Justin decided . . . Decided what?

Deborah got up and carefully opened the casement door. Looking as casual as possible in case she should be overlooked, she strolled out on to the terrace.

Nobody moved. Nobody hurried out behind her, or came warningly in off the grass or around a corner. She walked down the steps and round the building, keeping well away from the walls; though it was inconceivable that there should be another collapse of masonry.

The stables were deserted. She waited on the edge of the yard for as long as she could bear, to make sure that no groom or stable boy was working or taking his ease in some secluded corner. The dappled mare on which she had at times ridden out with Justin whinnied. When she reached it, it nuzzled her and snuffled happily as she threw the saddle on it. Then there was the anguish of crossing the yard again, this time accompanied by hoofs clicking on the stones.

They were out of the yard. She led the mare off the path on to the grass, and mounted. At last glance up at the row of upper windows, in any one of which she expected to see a startled face, and then she urged the horse forward. Muffling the sound by keeping off the drive, on the grass beneath the limes, she lay sometimes along the animal's neck to avoid a swinging storm-tossed branch.

Outside the gates, the wind was fiercer than she had bargained for. The horse reared and made a move to turn back. Deborah fought her to a standstill, murmured, coaxed, and started her off across the breck. They kept a steady pace, but the mare's head jerked spasmodically from side to side. The sand was biting at her eyes, just as at Deborah's.

Now they were well away from Stannard Priory they could keep to the road. It made a gritty smear through the haze ahead, wavering on into the tawny bracken and the sand-whipped clumps of ling. For a while it narrowed between two miniature dunes which had not been here a few days earlier, then broadened again towards the crossroads.

Deborah took the road along the ridge which would begin, two miles from here, to dip and turn towards Saxwold Hall.

The gale was in jubilant form up here. It forced her head down, so that she watched only the road and the protesting shudders of the mare's neck and flanks. Sand began to race in fine layers across the road, floating inches above the ground so that height was distorted and Deborah felt herself in danger of sinking.

There were no landmarks. The sand was not thick; one felt that it would be easy to reach through it and touch something solid, but such solid shapes as there were had been blotted out. The whole world was a monotonous swirling brown.

Where the road went down into a shallow dip, there was a drift which the horse could not plod through. Deborah guided her gently round, to find another treacherous undulation of shifting, unstable hummocks. They had to pick their way round the outskirts of this range; to find the road had disappeared. It was to her right. No, it must be to the left. She ought to be heading straight for the clump of pines beside the next junction, and after that the route was straightforward. But there was no clump of pines visible.

Her alarm communicated itself to the mare. Neighing, it tugged round and began to flounder through a patch of scrub. Deborah was swung to one side as one hoof went into a rut, then tugged the animal's head round again. A sudden gust filled her eyes with sand, and she clung on blindly. The mare broke into a mad gallop.

They were racing through a dry fog towards some unimaginable precipice.

The land here was flat and stony, but the faster they went the more it seemed to tilt, until they were racing headlong down that dizzying slope.

And all at once the slope was reversed, the ground was rushing up at her, and at the same time sliding sideways up another incline. Deborah hit a tussock of spiny grass and rolled over twice, her arms thrown up over her head.

By the time she had scrambled up, the mare was a dark ghost blending into the brown curtain until it was completely swallowed up. Deborah turned her back to the wind and tried desperately to peer into the distance and force some tree or bush out of it.

There was nothing.

She had to choose. She must set herself a direction as well as she could, and once started on it must not lose heart. Not downhill. By her estimate, the ridge had a fair way to go before it began to slope towards Saxwold Hall. She must keep parallel with the road, even if she was quite unable to find the road itself.

She turned so that the storm raged

against her right temple, and with bowed head began to plod forward. Her ankle was hurting. She forced herself on.

Abruptly the ground shelved away into a little pit. Trying to stop herself on the wrong foot, to avoid jarring down on the aching ankle, she stumbled. The rim of the pit dissolved beneath her. For an instant her left foot was caught in a rabbit hole; then there was a crack, and she was free, and rolling down over a stabbing, scraping litter of flints.

This time there was no doubt about it: her ankle was broken.

14

Near to fainting with the pain, Deborah dragged herself inch by inch up the side of the pit. At the top she let herself slump over the crumbling lip, hating the bite of agony and the bite of the wind. It would be so much easier to slide back into shelter again and let the storm spend itself over her head.

As in a mirage, she had a picture of the map she had consulted before first setting out for this place. Such a small area, featureless and un-alarming on its linen background: a compact wilderness. From where she now lay, it had the dimensions of the most terrifying desert, a limitless Sahara where she would drown in sand.

If she crawled on, seeking help, she might at last come across a warrener. In spite of the storm they might be about their business. They must know what was practical and what was not; must have

acclimatised themselves through generations of work on the breck. And if by now
she had crossed the border of Randall
Gaunt's land . . .

She dragged herself along a few yards.
Pinned to the ground like this, she found
the breck even more cruel than it looked:
a torture of flint and sand and grit, of
scrub and rasping grasses, of molehills
and rabbit holes and suddenly a tree root.
A pine leaned above her, away from the
wind. She set her back against it and
gulped for breath. Each gulp rasped her
throat with sand particles. The tree shook
with the throb of the wind. A vibration
seemed to run through the ground itself.
In the immeasurable distance there was a
steadier rhythm; but it could all be part of
the storm's assault, punching the air
above and around her.

Another shape formed out of the haze.
She blinked at it, wondering what trick it
would play on her eyes this time. It took
on substance. There was the rasp of a
hoof against loose flint. Two horses bore
slowly down upon her.

'Here — over here.'

Deborah tried to drag herself up by holding on to the tree trunk.

One of the horses, riderless, was the dappled mare. It was meek enough now, led on a loose rein by the rider of a large black stallion. The rider was Harry Chevening. The collar of his bottle-green cutaway was turned up about his neck, and the peak of his tweed cap pulled well down over his eyes. Even so he managed to look jaunty — a jauntiness that increased when he saw Deborah huddled below him.

'Upon my word! There's some bright plumage on the banks today.' He swung down from the saddle and tethered the two horses to the tree. 'You'll need many a month learning the breck paths before you travel in such a blow, dear lady.'

'I'll not be travelling this way again.'

He put out his hand to her. She took it; but when he tried to pull her up, her leg crumpled and she almost fell into his arms.

'A moment, now.' He balanced her against his shoulder, smiling insolently, and looked down at the foot she was

298

endeavouring to keep off the ground. 'What befell you?'

'Mr. Chevening, if you'll be kind enough to help me remount, I'll be on my way.'

'On your way?' he said. 'With a sprained ankle? Or is it more than that?'

Carefully he lowered her to the ground, and his fingers probed the ankle. She flinched, more from his touch than from the pain. With a derisive grunt he took off his jacket, and after three savage tugs succeeded in tearing a sleeve from his shirt. He bound it tightly about her ankle, then put his arm under her shoulders again.

'Now we'll be on our way.' He helped her towards the mare. 'But I'll choose the route.'

'I have an appointment. I'm indebted to you, but I'm sure I shall be capable of continuing my own journey now.'

'Do you know north from south?' he mocked. 'East from west? Duke's Plantation from Tinker's Clump?'

'I shall find my way.' She swayed in the saddle.

'I'll find it for you.'

She longed to dismiss him. But he was unlikely to leave her now. Very well, then: he must escort her to Saxwold Hall. His reaction to such a request would most likely be one of sardonic reproach, and there was no telling what story he would make of it when he met Justin again.

Mutely she allowed him to take charge. They jogged along in silence for a while. She concentrated on adjusting each movement to the hang of her bandaged ankle, clenching her teeth and willing herself not to sob.

After a while Chevening said: 'When you're used to our ways, I fancy you'll enjoy life in the breckland.'

'My ideas of enjoyment differ from yours, Mr. Chevening.'

'Ah, we all have something to learn from one another.'

The throb in her ankle became a savage pulse. It goaded her into saying: 'Is that what you and your cronies told my maid? And those other girls before her — and Beatrice? Was Beatrice forced to *learn* from you?'

His crooked grin showed how hugely he was enjoying himself. 'She was not my personal pupil. And the past is the past, dear lady. Let's concern ourselves with your future. Tell me — '

'There was something,' said Deborah. 'I know it. Something Beatrice did, or Edwin did.'

'It wasn't what Edwin did,' said Chevening offhandedly. 'It was what he didn't do.'

'You lured him into gambling.'

'He came very readily, I assure you.'

'You used him, cheated him . . . '

Chevening slowed and turned to face her. She could not have foreseen such cold, righteous indignation in a man of his depraved character.

'My friends and I, madam, are men of honour. Cheating is not among our pastimes. We play fairly and we pay our debts.'

'That is your definition of honour?'

'It will serve. And we expect others to honour their bargains, or their boasts. Edwin didn't win his last throw. But give his memory its due: he met his obligations. That's all one asks of one's fellows — but dammit, one does *ask* it.'

The storm was slackening. She could raise her head, sit more comfortably, and talk without having to turn away from the wind. Gouts of sand puffed up from the ground, but about her shoulders it was dying away to a thin, dry drizzle.

'What do you mean when you say Edwin didn't win? What was the wager?'

'I'll say no more, Lady Stannard.'

'I am not Lady Stannard.'

'But soon will be.'

'Mr. Chevening, if you think that after what I witnessed two evenings ago, I would contemplate marrying a man of such bestial tastes — '

'A bachelor must have his diversions. You'll find his experiences have made him all the better as a husband, I'll warrant you.'

'Not a husband to suit my tastes.'

'Oh, come now. You disappoint me. I took you for a travelled lady who knows damn well what life is like. Life as it is, ma'am, and not as it's portrayed in the volumes of a circulating library. Justin's as

302

good a man as the next, and you'll do very well with him. You know what he wants, and you have the advantage of him, for you know also the thing he wants without knowing it, so you can decide what the mixture is to be. You forbid this pleasure and grant that, as it suits you.'

'You would call that a persuasive argument?'

'It's a true one, Lady Stannard.'

'I tell you I am not Lady Stannard.'

'I find it natural to be respectful in advance of the actual ceremony.'

There will be no ceremony. I am not, and will not be, Lady Stannard. I have told Lord Stannard so. I've made it known beyond all possibility of doubt.'

'Have you, now? Then,' said Chevening, 'our young baron has been lying to me. He's been telling me it's as good as settled.'

'As a horseman, Mr. Chevening, you well know what goes before a fall.'

Scattered trees were emerging from the thinning haze. She knew now where they were. Another ten minutes more, and Stannard Priory would come into view.

Before it was too late, she had to make her companion say what else there was to say.

'Justin has lost a fortune to you?' she hazarded.

'The luck of the game. He won from Edwin, now it's his own turn: he has lost. Another day the wheel may turn.'

'He has lost. And is in debt to you?'

'Considerably so.'

'You'll keep on until everyone is destroyed but yourself?'

'Someone may destroy me first. That's half the excitement of the game.'

He was trying to quicken their pace, but Deborah slowed deliberately. She felt lightheaded. The idea of what she was about to do seemed both impossible and inevitable. She made herself stare at Chevening, until he was aware of the provocation in her gaze. He matched the pace of his horse to hers, and smiled warily; but his conceit was too great, he responded, emitting a soundless whistle and obviously framing some insolent remark.

Deborah said: 'Would you risk a wager with me, sir?'

'Well, I'll be damned.'

'Probably. But you have not answered my question.'

'This is hardly the time or the place.'

'I thought that gamblers were always ready to try their luck.'

He laughed. 'How very tantalising you are . . . Miss Ritchie. Very well. What shall we play for?'

'I want the full story of what happened to my sister.'

'Oh-ho.' He rode slowly on, wagging his head. 'No, that's not for me to say.'

'You're afraid?'

'It was none of my business, and still is not.'

'You won't risk the throw?'

The angry pride she had detected before came back into the tightening line of his jaw and cheekbones. Quietly he asked: 'What stake do *you* offer?'

'A kiss.' Her tone was hushed.

'A kiss,' he said. 'Young woman, you're a fraud. Damn, what a fraud! You play the prim little puritan, full of high principles and disgust for we poor brutish men — and now you're gambling with your favours and . . . and . . . ' Words failed him.

Deborah said: 'But I shall not be called on to pay.'

'Ah. You're not expecting to lose?'

'No.'

'You amaze me the more every second, Miss Ritchie.'

If she lost — and for all her bravado she knew it was as likely as winning — she would have to taste that lascivious, loathsome mouth. She looked at the twist of his lips; and he knew she was looking, and laughed.

'Well?' she said.

'You wouldn't consider raising the stake? Justin had a much better . . . ' He checked himself, but his gaze raked her body. 'In your present state, you are hardly capable of resisting any demand I might make — if I enforced it, eh?'

'You spoke of being a man of honour. For a moment I was foolish enough to believe there might be some merit in you.'

'You put me in an invidious position, ma'am.'

'A mere kiss is not worth your stake. So

let us forget the matter.'

She urged the mare forward but he leaned over to catch the rein and draw them closer.

'If you win, and all I have to tell you is that there is nothing to be told about Beatrice — nothing that *I* can tell?'

'I shall honour my side of the bargain. I can only trust you to do the same.'

She was shocked to realise that in a way she was enjoying the duel. It was shameful. But she must go through with it now, and she must win.

They came to a halt. 'I carry no dice, or cards. Not on a day such as this. What shall it be — I will toss a coin, or you will roll stones in the gully over there? Or . . . ?'

'I prefer not to get down.' Deborah studied the ground by her horse's hoofs. Then she pointed. 'That stone — a small eye stone, is it not?'

Chevening slid from his horse and picked up the stone. It was little more than an inch across, but there was a neat hole right through its centre. 'You think this will bring you luck?'

'I fancy it. That, and an ordinary flint.'

He found a stone of about the same size and held them both out for her inspection. 'How shall we play, then?'

'One in each hand, behind your back,' she said steadily. 'Hold them out in your fists. And if I pick the hand with the eye stone, then I win.'

He looked at the stones in his open palms. 'Rather abrupt. Shall we make it three guesses? Two out of three to win. You'll find it adds spice to the contest.'

Without waiting for further argument, Chevening put his hands behind his back. He stood still for an eternity, tormenting her. His eyes were bright. He stared at her lips as he brought his hands out and held the clenched fists up to her. Deborah felt the horse fidget beneath her.

Abruptly she tapped Chevening's right hand. He opened it. The stone inside was the plain flint.

'Aren't you glad we settled for three?'

She stared above his head towards the horizon. It was appearing now, the faintest blur of a line between dusty sky and dusty earth.

Chevening's fists were raised again. Without pausing to think or to allow herself fear, she chose the right hand again. He revealed the eye stone.

Both of them took long, deep breaths. 'You see?' cried Chevening exultantly. 'Can you truthfully tell me you're not stirred by this?' He took a malicious age for the last choice, before brandishing his fists at her.

Deborah hesitated.

'There!' he crowed. 'Now you're appreciating the finer points. Draw it out — make me wait! Now you're learning what it was like for Justin, and Edwin . . . for all of us.'

She struck his left hand as if to draw blood.

Slowly he opened it. The eye stone seemed to wink at her.

*   *   *

'Edwin's last stake,' said Chevening, 'was Beatrice.'

Deborah swayed in the saddle. Chevening put out a hand to her, but she forced herself to sit upright. With a mocking curl of those lips that she surely could not have hated more if she had lost, he swung up into his own saddle. They moved on at a leisurely pace. He savoured every sentence: she had won, but she should suffer for it.

'Edwin had lost his money, as you guessed. Lost it to Justin, on one of Justin's lucky streaks.'

'And lost his wife's money as well?'

'The same thing, is it not?'

'And when all Beatrice's money was gone . . . ?'

'Then Justin, in the most sporting spirit one can conceive, offered him a last chance to recoup. A week of Beatrice's company against the return of all Edwin's losses so far. Deucedly decent, I'd say.'

'And Edwin lost.'

'Edwin lost, yes. So Beatrice was accommodated for a week in the Stannard vault. I've no reason to suppose that Justin did not — ah — take good care of her during that idyll.'

Stannard Priory was a roofline of crenellations, turrets and chimneys ahead.

Deborah stared at it, not trusting herself to look her contempt at Chevening. She said: 'So that's what killed her.'

'I doubt it. I very much doubt it. Your sister had appetites of her own — '

'Enough! I'll not listen to another word. How dare you defile her memory?'

Chevening shrugged. The picture was hideously clear. After a week of humiliation in that accursed vault, the ravaged Beatrice would have gone despairingly home to Toft Warren House, there to find Edwin sodden with drink — and with remorse, if that was in him. What could they have found to say to each other: what possible promises could there have been for the future? Their deaths could have been a pact of self-annihilation, of eternal forgetfulness.

As they rode into the avenue, Chevening said: 'You can't bring your sister back. But if revenge amuses you, you can make Justin pay.'

'How?'

'By marrying him, and choosing how best to torment him. As I observed earlier, you are the one who can call the

311

tune. It might be amusing to watch.'

'I understood you were his friend.'

'We shall be a sight friendlier when he pays me what he owes.'

'Which is your only real reason for favouring our marriage.' They were approaching the gateway. Deborah tried a last impulsive thrust. 'Which of you killed Miriam? And what drove that other poor girl to hang herself?'

'I'm afraid I know nothing of such misfortunes,' said Chevening. 'And if I did, they were not part of our wager.'

He was helping her down, taking her weight so that her left foot should not touch the ground, as Justin came out.

'Taking the dapple out, riding off into *that* . . . on such a day!' Justin's rancour was as shrill as a woman's. 'What possessed you? What — '

'Your betrothed,' said Chevening, 'has sustained a broken ankle.'

Justin's anger ebbed, overrun by a current of gloating pity. 'Broken, now? I did entreat you to rest. And now . . . ' He turned and bellowed something into the hall. After the briefest delay two men hurried out to help Deborah up the steps and indoors. 'You're decidedly not fit to travel *now*, my dear,' said Justin.

As she was carried carefully upstairs she saw, through the banisters, Justin opening the library door and leading Harry Chevening in. She wondered how much Chevening would say and how he would use it; and what Justin would make of it.

She was laid on her bed. Kirstie had already been summoned, and helped her gingerly out of her coat, loosened her bodice, and lamented, 'Oh, miss, whatever have you done this time?'

Deborah found that even in dragging herself up so that she could be propped against pillows she was communicating a wrench and sickening pain to her ankle.

'You'll be needing a doctor, Miss Deborah.'

'I wish Sir Randall Gaunt to be sent for.'

Kirstie made sure she was settled as well as could be managed, and went out. Deborah stared impotently out of the window. The wind grumbled fitfully away, a half-subdued animal still ready to start another tussle. The sky, clearing of the sand pall, was a sullen crimson.

When Kirstie tiptoed back into the room, her eyes avoided Deborah's. 'His lordship has that friend of his in there. I didnae fancy interrupting them. But I had a wee word with Miss Isabel, and she'll be passing it on. Though I'd no say she looked too happy about that Sir Randall.'

Deborah said: 'Kirstie, I want you to tell me the truth about the drink you brought me last night. And this time I'd like you to describe what really took place.'

Kirstie moaned.

'Whose idea was it?' Deborah insisted. 'And what was in the drink?'

'I didn't make it up, miss.'

'It was meant to make me sleep, wasn't it? Laudanum, or some such thing? Meant to make sure we missed this morning's train.'

'I should never ha' been brought to this place,' wailed the girl. 'That place they got me into, and the things they did . . .'

'You seemed to enjoy it well enough.'

'Miss, that was the liquor speaking. Some of the things they kindled there, they were terrible . . . aye, terrible. Ye shouldnae ha' brought us here, miss.'

Deborah said: 'Lord Stannard ordered you to give me that drink?'

'He meant no harm,' quavered Kirstie. 'That he swore. Said he meant you nothing but good, and wanted you to stay so that he'd have another chance of talking to you, and I'd best be helping him.'

'And if you didn't?'

'Miss, if you took me straight home there'd be Mr. MacKenzie, and how was I to fare once *he'd* heard? But if I did what was asked, I'd be well looked after. He promised.'

'And if you didn't?' asked Deborah again.

'He . . . that place . . . he said I'd no get away, and I'd be taken back there, and there'd been a lass was frightened to death, and it'd nae be that much trouble to frighten *me* to death.'

'Frightened to death. Yes, I see.'

'Miss, ye'd no let on I've been telling you all this?'

There was a knock at the door. Kirstie let out a squeak of dread.

Justin came in. His glance drove Kirstie from the room. He stood at the foot of Deborah's bed. 'What's this absurd message I've received?'

'My only message was one asking for a doctor.'

'Naturally you shall have one. As soon as we are sure the Meddleheath road is clear, I'll send for Abbott.'

'I wish Sir Randall Gaunt to attend me.'

'He'll not set foot in this house.' He was hard and complacent. 'I know what is best, and I'll not have that charlatan tampering with you.'

She wondered if Chevening had related all that had passed between them, making a characteristically obscene joke of it. And all too probably Justin had guessed, the moment he entered this room, that Kirstie had babbled out her own frag-ments of the truth. None of it would please him. She knew too much now, and guessed more. But to shout defiance at him might be to set off something she could not control.

He waited for a few seconds as if tempting her to speak. Then, with a little nod of self-congratulation, he left.

No doctor arrived. No one other than Kirstie came near. And Kirstie was answering no more questions: this time, thought Deborah, because she knew none of the answers.

There could be no real danger from Justin. He surely sustained no lingering hope of marrying her, but that didn't mean he was angry enough to kill her. Even the fear of what she might say about him once she was free was insufficient grounds for murder. So she kept assuring herself.

A scandal about his conduct in the priory was something he could suppress. Deferential supporters would rally around him. Accusations would trickle away to nothingness. But murder — no, widely as his writ might run in this neighbourhood, he surely would not go that far. He did not *need* to go that far. Unless he had more to be afraid of than she yet knew. And unless he was madder than she had allowed herself to realise.

Alone in the night, Deborah inched painfully across the bed. By bracing herself against the bedknob she could lean far enough out to clutch the back of the armchair facing the window. She swung herself over and collapsed into the chair. With her right foot she was able to edge it round to command a view of the door.

At least she would meet her attacker face to face. She was not going to lie down and wait meekly. She would not risk sleep.

Several times her head nodded and she twitched awake. She tried to stay awake by watching the grass outside, leaning to the left so that she could see across the park and the trees to that stone claw of the ruins. Once she fancied she saw a light, but it was a fancy to which she was all too prone by now.

The sky brightened with a distant splash of lightning. The sandstorm had given way to a sultry stillness, through which the muttering of thunder replaced the dying fret of the wind. It was coming closer. The trees stirred uneasily. Out of the storm-glow of the breck a pheasant screamed harshly.

Lightning forked out of the heavens. Trees and bushes were vividly outlined for a second, then faded back into huddled shadow.

Deborah's chin dropped forward. No one would come. She was in no danger. Her fears were half of her own making.

There was an ear-splitting crack. Her instinctive movement sent jagged lightning through her ankle.

Far out on the breck there was a red tongue, licking up into the sky. Gradually, as she watched, a sullen glow spread along the ridge. Shadows took on new form. Somewhere the dry heath had caught fire, and the blaze would soon spread. The whole horizon was rimmed with pulsating shades of smeared red and orange, topped by thickening tufts of smoke, by the time she heard hoofbeats on the far side of the house. A thump and shuffle of activity downstairs was followed by the sound of more horses riding away.

Lightning scythed again. It was leaving the heath and seeking new victims in the heart of the estate. Successive flashes were accompanied by a cannonade of thunder, shaking through the house. Deborah watched spellbound. Yellow smoke rolled across the ridges, and in the foreground the trees were bathed in light, dropped back into gloom, then plucked dazzlingly out again.

In the middle of the night inferno, there came one great flash of lightning so close that Deborah felt it tingle down the backs of her hands and down the back of her neck. For a glaring instant it was pinned to the last pinnacle of the priory ruins.

From where she sat, she could not tell the time on her bedside clock. There must be many hours to dawn, but from now on there was no real darkness. Her eyes ached with tiredness and with the intermittent glare of the lightning. One more bolt seemed to strike somewhere near; then there was a lull. Now she could smell the acridness of the smoke.

The storm rolled away, the flames drew no closer. Deborah put her head back and closed her eyes. Justin would surely be far away, lending his authority to the fire-fighters on the heath. Nobody would come tonight. She drowsed, awoke at dawn, and drowsed off again.

Only when Kirstie had brought a breakfast tray and she had finished eating did she realise that something was missing. The last remnant of the priory's window arch no longer crooked above the trees.

15

'Kirstie, there are some walking sticks in a stand by the hall door. Bring me the stoutest you can find, will you?'

'Miss, ought you to be up and about?'

'Please do as I say, Kirstie.'

If Justin were in the house and saw the girl . . . Deborah sighed with relief when the door opened to reveal Kirstie with a silver-handled ebony cane. She was just in time. A few minutes later, a door slammed downstairs and a man's footsteps tramped across the hall; and Justin was calling something. She heard him come upstairs, and waited for as long as she could endure before setting out towards the landing. Even with the aid of the stick she could not prevent little twists and sways of her ankle. But she reached the main staircase, leaned for a moment against the turn of the banisters, and looked down at the tiled floor of the hall.

There was a movement behind her. She

turned. Justin was striding at her as though nothing now could stop him. She gripped the banister rail and swung her stick up like a lance.

He came to within an inch of its ferrule. 'Be careful. In your present unsteady condition, you may too easily have an accident.'

'You'd hope to make it look like an accident?'

He advanced a cautious step. The ferrule touched his chest. 'What sort of monster do you take me for?' He was as handsome as Lucifer, and as destructive, now. It could not be disguised: she saw in his eyes that he meant her, now or as soon as he had the opportunity, to die. It was terrifying in its senselessness.

Below, Isabel came into the hall and looked up.

Justin stepped to one side and offered Deborah his arm. She brushed it aside, gripped the stick, and eased herself down from one step to the next.

'Should you be moving about?' said Isabel.

'Of course she should not.' Justin

sounded his old self. 'But we've discovered how capricious she is, have we not?'

'The fire,' said Isabel. 'Is it under control?'

'I didn't leave until I thought it safe. We'll need to leave the beaters on watch for the rest of the day, but I don't see it spreading.'

'The roof of the cheese-press has collapsed. It must have been that noise I heard at about two o'clock.'

'I noticed that when I went through the stableyard.'

'And the priory,' said Deborah. She edged herself towards the long settle below the stairs, and lowered herself warily on to it.

'What about the priory?' asked Isabel.

'The ruins must be a bit more ruined by now. Lightning struck the window arch.'

Justin towered over her. 'You're sure of this?' The turmoil of indecision in his eyes was very nearly as disturbing as his naked hatred. He did not want to believe. Then he said:

'I will go to see what damage has been done.'

Deborah said: 'You're afraid some of your playthings may have been damaged?'

It was foolish to provoke him. If she had not been seated, leaning forward on her stick, she felt he might conceivably have struck her before hurrying out of the hall.

'It's far from comfortable here,' said Isabel. 'Lean on me, and we'll go into the small salon.'

Deborah allowed herself to be helped up, then stood her ground. 'You must help me to leave. I must get away.'

'But you mustn't travel in your present state. Until you've seen the doctor — '

'Who will never come.'

'Justin has been busy with the fire. First the sandstorm on the heath, then the fire — it's a heavy responsibility.'

Deborah said: 'I no longer feel safe with your brother. I think I am better away from here, as soon as possible. Please. I implore you, Isabel, help me.'

Isabel gulped. Instead of replying she tried to take Deborah's arm and guide her towards a door opening out of the hall. Deborah rammed the stick against the floor, into a crack between tiles.

'When you've had a good rest,' Isabel was saying unhappily, 'when you've seen the doctor and Justin has found it safe to drive across the breck — '

'Safe?' Deborah was closer to tears than she had realised. 'It is *here* I am not safe.'

There was the swish of carriage wheels on the drive, and the slowing clop of horses drawing up within the gateway.

'Offers of help in fighting the fire.' Isabel was glad of an excuse to change the subject. 'Or requests for help somewhere else.'

They heard the faint rasp of the bell wire under the porch. Isabel waited, expecting the door to be opened on some familiar local face and to have to explain Justin's whereabouts.

When the butler pulled it back, General Fleming stood in the entrance.

Deborah was overpowered by a great rush of thankfulness. The old man was stooped and frail, but all at once she felt she had a protector. She began to hobble towards him without waiting for the butler's announcement.

Fleming stared. 'Bless me soul, what have you been doing, my girl?'

Isabel came past Deborah. 'I'm afraid you find the household in some confusion, General. My brother — '

'Seen a doctor?' barked Fleming.

'There has been no opportunity so far,' said Deborah. 'I only broke it yesterday, and what with the storm and everything else . . .'

Don't ask too many questions, she silently entreated. *Don't ruffle the surface, please, just take me away from here without any fuss. Take me away, please, let it be all right for me to get away before Justin returns.*

Fleming said: 'A fine pair of crocks, we two.' Coming into the middle of the hall he compared his gnarled stick with Deborah's smooth ebony one. 'Well, I must say, I've come at the right time.'

'I thought, sir,' said Isabel, 'that you had already gone back to . . . Bath, wasn't it?'

'Suffered a bit of a setback. Gaunt's

treating me. Wouldn't let me go until he was satisfied.'

'But Sir Randall is no longer permitted to practise.'

'Choose my own healer, thank'ee. I judge by results.' He smiled at Deborah, his eyes steady and commanding. 'Recommend him. Just what you need. Look at me, girl — a bit groggy, I'll admit, but fit enough to make me own way here today. With the aid of a coachman who knows every inch of the way,' he added with a disarming twinkle at Isabel.

Isabel was not disarmed. 'To attempt it when the roads must be still difficult — what could be so urgent?'

'We had little trouble. I came,' he said to Deborah, 'to take you to inspect the siting of the new lectern.'

'General,' Isabel protested. 'It is not so many days since Miss Ritchie was arbitrarily summoned to Saxwold Hall on such an excuse, and now — '

'Now,' Fleming eagerly took her up, 'I am well enough to leave, and want to settle each last detail. I have come to fetch Miss Ritchie to Saxwold Hall. And seeing the state of her foot, I think I chose the right time to come.'

'I'm sure my brother would insist that she remains until Dr. Abbott can get here.'

'And when will that be?'

'There have been so many alarms during the night. Now that the fire is under control, and if the doctor can get through — '

'I got through,' said Fleming. 'And I shall get back. If Miss Ritchie comes with me, she will be in good hands.'

Deborah said: 'Isabel, you know I must go. Unless you're deliberately keeping me prisoner, you will let me go.'

'What nonsense.'

'Yes, nonsense,' said the general bluffly. 'Nobody's keeping you prisoner, m'dear. You're free to come and go as you choose. Eh, Miss Stannard?'

Isabel looked at Deborah.

Deborah said quietly: 'Isabel, I wonder if you'd be kind enough to fetch Kirstie for me.'

There was a petrified moment. Then Isabel hurried away. Even now, Deborah thought as she gripped the handle of her stick tightly, it could be too late. If Isabel played for time, delaying or simply hiding herself away without saying a word to Kirstie, if Justin came back over the grass and into the house before they could be down the drive and away . . .

Kirstie appeared alone. Perhaps if Isabel saw nothing further, did not witness their departure, she would find it easier to lie to her brother.

'Miss, we're not leaving just the way we — '

'We're leaving,' said General Fleming, 'now.'

They were at the door when Lady Stannard appeared on the landing above.

'This commotion. Whatever is going on? Justin?' She leaned over the rail, wrinkling her nose. Ludicrously Deborah felt that they ought to wait for her to come downstairs so that there could be formal goodbyes and thanks.

With Kirstie on one side to help her, she followed General Fleming to Randall Gaunt's carriage.

They gathered speed along the lime

avenue. They were out of the gates and turning. This was the last time, this must be the last time, she would be borne along this road.

She put her head back against the leather and sighed. The tang of smoke and burnt grass became stronger. Suddenly she said: 'If we're going to Meddleheath first, to the church, we ought to have turned off just there.'

'No intention of going to the church,' said Fleming. 'Had to spin some kind of yarn, m'dear. Same as last time, I admit, but what else was there to say? Phew.' He patted Kirstie on the knee, and she stared at him, awestruck. 'Afraid we might not get away with it. Too old for this kind of thing. Couldn't put up much of a fight at my time of life.'

'What made you think there might be a fight?' Deborah marvelled.

'Knew you were in danger — had to get you out. Gaunt couldn't come himself. Bound to cause trouble — never get you away. In any case, he's got his hands full at the moment.'

Despite sand drifts beside the road and

leaking out across it, and air full of drifting flecks of burnt grass and leaves, the coachman was making good time. An occasional rut jarred Deborah's ankle, but she didn't mind. They could surely not catch her now. Choked with gratitude, she leaned forward to put her hand over the general's. 'I think you're the most wonderful man.'

Fleming cleared his throat. 'I haven't had anything like that said to me, in that tone of voice, for years . . . One thing,' he added, 'the fellow can't have found out yet, or he wouldn't have risked letting you get away. Wouldn't have left you alone for a second. Hasn't been to the ruins yet, eh?'

'He was there when you arrived.'

'My God.' Fleming wiped his brow. 'Even closer shave than I thought.'

'Why should you have supposed me in danger? And what do the ruins have to do with it?'

'Leave it to Gaunt to explain. Seems to make some sense to him, in a ghastly sort of way. Not to me.'

When they slowed to turn in through

the gates of Saxwold Hall, Deborah noticed to her surprise two huge eye stones at the base of the gateposts.

'Don't tell me Sir Randall's trying to keep evil spirits at bay?'

Fleming snorted. 'Spotted 'em on my way out. Not young Randall's doing. More likely some of those superstitious yokels thinking to keep *his* evil influence within his own grounds.' At length, despite his disability, he was able to hand her gently down from the carriage when it stopped before the hall.

Randall Gaunt strode to meet her. The once cold grey house was alive with his presence. His hands were outstretched. There was a moment of self-restraint, then the gap between them closed, and she was in his arms. It was unthinkable, but it was utterly right and natural.

He released her, then caught her again to steady her as he became aware of her awkwardness and the stick that was in danger of sliding away. 'But what's this? What's been done to you?'

He was supporting her into his study. She let herself sink unashamedly into the cradle of his arm. When he made her lie on a sofa while he replaced the ankle bandage with a leather support, the touch of his fingers was a blissful pain. He raised his head and abruptly, almost angrily, his lips sought hers.

'I've thought of you since we first met, without at first knowing it.' He drew back. 'But this is too fast for you. To you I'm still a stranger, eccentric and unreliable.'

'Not unreliable. And no stranger. I don't know how all this can be, but I shall find out why, in time.'

'We shall find out together. But first there's something you must know.' His arm was about her again and he brought her to her feet. Leaning on him, she had no wish to move. Gently he said: 'You must be prepared for a shock. You've had no inkling?'

'Of what?'

'Of Justin Stannard's revenant: of the young woman now in my care?'

'Another one? Another one of the old stories about you and this house — about the young women you keep hidden away?'

'This time,' he said, 'the story is true.'

He led her upstairs, half turned to lift her by the elbow from one step to another. They went along a short passage and he stopped at a bedroom door. Briefly he faltered, then he opened the door and helped her through.

Deborah went in. There was a four-poster bed with its head to the wall, the curtains drawn back. A woman lay on it, staring up at the hangings. The sound of the opening door reached her, and she turned her head as Deborah took a couple of steps closer to the bed.

The face was disfigured by anguish and illness, but there was no mistaking it. The woman was Beatrice.

16

'From the moment she reached us this morning, we knew you could be in danger,' said Randall, 'once he found out. Thank God the ruse worked.'

Beatrice looked yearningly at Deborah, trying to smile. As she turned her head on the pillow, Deborah could see the blisters and discolourations of a wide burn up her neck and behind her ear, where the light sandy hair had been scorched away.

'Deborah.' It was a pitiful croak.

Deborah bent over the bed. She had not expected to see this face again; nor that she should see it so drained and distorted. Suddenly she kissed Beatrice's forehead, and Beatrice groped a feeble arm thankfully about her shoulder.

With the greatest tenderness, Randall helped Beatrice to raise her head, easing another pillow into place. He examined her throat and her right arm, which, Deborah now saw, was severely bruised and glistening with ointment.

Randall straightened up. 'I'll leave you with her for a while. You'll have much to say. I'll come back in twenty minutes. If she tires before then, please pull the bell-rope.' He drew a basket chair to the bedside for Deborah, and left them together.

'You're alive.' It was all Deborah could say.

'Much better dead.'

'It's a sin even to think such a thing.'

'I've committed so many sins. What is one more?'

'There's so much to ask,' said Deborah. 'I've been mystified about that letter you sent me before you . . . and now, well, now here you are. But how *did* you get here — and where have you been all this time?'

'You must have had a lot of trouble because of me,' Beatrice said humbly. 'I owe you an explanation . . . I'm so glad to see you. I never thought to see you again.'

Her eyes misted over, and for a moment Deborah was concerned that she might be fainting, and reached for the bell-pull. But Beatrice was looking back into the terrible past. She began to describe it in a flat, emotionless voice which every now and then quickened to agony and sobbed away again. She had no pride left and made no excuses. It was a bleak, bitter confession for which she expected no absolution.

*　*　*

When the Flemings came to Toft Warren House they had at first been frequent visitors to Saxwold Hall, and Sir Randall Gaunt had several times accepted invitations to dine with them. Beatrice admitted that she had been strongly attracted to him. It had become a challenge — difficult to resist — to coax him flirtatiously out of his devotion to work. She was at her most outrageous when Isabel Stannard was present, demonstrating the ways of charming a man: in conversation, in attentiveness, or a sparkle of the eye, a finger laid thoughtfully on the throat by her

338

neckline, an admiring laugh at the right moment.

But gradually they came to see less and less of Gaunt. He had seemed for a while to want a fuller social life, then gave up and sank back into his old pursuits. He was happier in his shell and wished to share it with nobody. He spent more and more time in London. She and Edwin began to spend more time with the Stannards.

Beatrice had found Justin, too, attractive. But fencing with him, you could be seriously hurt. Flirtation might be turned into something else. She sensed the danger of being drawn too close to Justin Stannard.

Edwin did not sense it in time. He was easy prey for Justin and Harry Chevening. Playing on his weakness for gambling, which had already caused a minor scandal in Bath and driven him and Beatrice from the city, they went through his remaining money. Running up debts and drinking heavily to keep up his courage, Edwin went insanely into battle with the money Beatrice had brought him. It took very little time for him to lose it.

'And then,' said Beatrice, 'he swore he would recoup it all on a last throw. A final gamble, with the last thing he had left to stake.'

'I know,' said Deborah softly. 'I pieced the story together from things I was told by Harry Chevening.'

Now Beatrice told in her resigned, emotionless voice of Justin's cruel pleasure in his triumph. He installed her in the priory with a great flourish of mock gallantry, showered derisive compliments on her.

'And came to me every night,' she said, 'like a ravenous animal.'

'But could you not have repudiated the whole shameful agreement? You were no party to the bet. You were Edwin's wife, not some soulless counter in an obscene game.'

'I had to honour it, for his sake. He could not have endured my existence as a . . . a bad debt. He pleaded with me. I've never before seen a man weep. If I would honour his bargain, he would always respect me for the sacrifice, he would make a life for us, a new life, he . . . ' For the first time her voice trembled and died in her throat.

Deborah said: 'Lie back. Close your eyes. We'll talk later.'

'No.' Beatrice rallied. As if to abase herself utterly, she went on: 'I was abominably used by Justin Stannard. The worst times were afterwards, when I wished to kill myself from shame.'

At last her sentence was ended. He drove her back to Toft Warren House. It was true, thought Deborah, that Justin had seen Beatrice returning home the day before the fire: he himself had set her down at her own front door and escorted her into an ill-kempt house deserted by everyone save Edwin.

Edwin was already incapable of speech. He must have been drinking steadily since Beatrice delivered herself up to Stannard Priory. Mrs. Pigle had left without his even being aware of it.

Justin made polite conversation, asking respectfully about Colonel Ritchie's death and the settlement of the estate. Beatrice told him as dismissively as possible that everything would go to her half-sister. She did not want his or Chevening's greedy eyes turning yet again to her and Edwin.

So Justin had been aware of Deborah's existence before the telegraph brought her name to him. If, so soon after his humiliation of Edwin, he in his turn suffered a heavy loss at Chevening's hands, then Deborah's arrival on the scene could have taken on quite a new significance.

She said: 'And when Justin had left? You and Edwin . . . and the fire . . . ?'

The worthlessness of Edwin's promises was soon evident. When Beatrice tried to comfort him, needing so much comfort herself, he thrust her away. He could not bear her to touch him. Wildly he accused her of having been soiled by Justin Stannard.

Their last quarrel flared up late at night on the first floor landing. The sudden terror of it came vividly through Beatrice's words. Edwin was carrying a lamp upstairs, filled with liquid fat in which floated a spluttering wick. Hot fat slopped against the sides of the deep saucer. At one moment he lurched against the banisters, and drops of fat congealed on the woodwork. Beatrice tried to take it from him. He refused to surrender it, and struck out at her. Then the lamp tipped over, he let go, and fat streamed over the banisters on to a dry, dusty tapestry fastened to the panelling below.

Flame rushed along the fabric and licked up through the banister rails. Its speed and ferocity were unbelievable. Beatrice was temporarily incapable of movement. She stared at the racing tongues of fire until she heard Edwin shout something and begin to run along the landing.

There was still time to brave the main staircase. But he stopped, paralysed. Jolted from her trance, Beatrice caught his arm and tried to urge him down, a step at a time. He put out a hand and gripped the rail, refusing to go on and afraid to turn back. Flame beat up under his fingertips and he let go and turned to hammer Beatrice's shoulders with his fists. She dodged to one side. A blast of heat swept across their faces. Edwin was obscured from her by smoke. One step forward and she seemed to be falling into the worst of the furnace. The rail gave way and she plunged down, rolling through smoke and past another scorching breath which became suddenly fiercer and seared agony up one side of her neck. Her hair was on fire. She beat it out as she stumbled to her feet. There was a crash behind her. Blazing woodwork tumbled into the hall. She thought Edwin was in the middle of it, a human torch; but so much was distorted that this might have been a figment of nightmare.

After it she remembered nothing for a long, long time.

She must have fought her way clear of the blaze, how she could not say. All her memory was of mounting pain, of being still in the heart of the fire. She must have stumbled away like a stricken beast, her mind shocked into insensibility.

Amidst it all, she had flashes of what she now knew to be reality. A man with a dark face bent over her and talked a language she could barely understand.

Then she was in a small room which rocked to and fro. Sunlight splashed across her eyes until he drew a lace curtain. Several times she tried to speak to the man who leaned over her or sat at a wooden chair, preparing food and strange mixtures in a wooden bowl. It was like trying to squeeze out words in a dream.

Other faces swam in and out, across a background of brightly painted walls and a gaudy sideboard built under the square side window. A dark, wizened old woman shook her head and talked in a repetitive sing-song.

Gradually the pain dimmed. The man rubbed strange-smelling salves into her burns, and there was a bitter drink which sent her off to sleep and into dreams which could not be separated from her waking dreams.

She was in a caravan. That she now understood. She began to focus her attention on the open door as they rumbled along, trying to guess from glimpses of trees and an occasional cottage roof where they were.

One day there was noise and jumbled

music. The man had shut the door and left her. When he returned he drew back the curtain and turned her face so that the light fell on it.

'You have a sister?'

'All at once I had such a clear picture of you,' she said to Deborah. 'I wanted to reach out to you, and wanted to tell him.'

All she could do was nod.

Again he went away, and a long time later came back and drew his wooden chair to the side of her bed. He said: 'Lord Stannard . . . ?'

She wanted to shake her head and deny that name, but all she managed was another vestige of a nod.

He began to talk earnestly in that slurred accent of his. She had been near to death's door and he had saved her, yes? It was not his fault he had not known what kind of lady she was. So burnt and ragged, how was he to know? But he had found her and looked after her and he meant no harm. It was a long time since his woman had died, he was alone and it had been good to bring her back to health. She would tell them how good he had been? It was in the middle of Lord Stannard's land he had found her, but she would please tell his lordship that he had not been poaching, it was an accident he had wandered off his usual road.

'I've seen the man!' Deborah exclaimed. 'He was at the races, and stared at me. He must have connected us. And Justin was there, and every vagabond on and off the breck knows Lord Stannard.'

'And fears him. But now he began to believe there might be some profit in it — a reward.'

Deborah could well imagine that the gypsy was more scared now of not taking Beatrice back than he had originally been of remaining in the neighbourhood.

So she was delivered, helpless, back to the one man she wanted above all others never to see again.

When Justin closed the entrance to the vault and stood at the foot of the steps, the shock of it burst through her speechlessness. A scream broke from her. She raved at him until she was hoarse.

'And after that,' said Beatrice stonily, 'it

was far worse in its way than the first time. For when he had recovered himself he began to make a sickly show of affection. He had been racked by remorse, he said, and had discovered that truly he loved me. My return was a miraculous second chance. He asked me to marry him.' She laughed the broken laugh she must have thrown at Justin when he put the grotesque question. 'And when I told him how I hated him and wanted only to die, he said I was already officially dead and would never be restored to life unless he wished it. He came to me again and again, one hour swearing he cared for me and would nurse me back to health and restore my lost memory — that was the story he proposed to make public in due course — and the next swearing I must do as he said or be left to rot. I found it most loathsome when he pretended affection.'

'And at the same time,' Deborah realised, 'he decided I must die. As the only surviving relative, you would then have my share of father's money as well as your own. That's what he wanted to get his hands on.'

Beatrice shrank down into the bed, her strength spent. Perhaps, in the priory, sheer exhaustion would have defeated her and Justin would have won the day in the end. But then came the storm.

When the arch of the window collapsed it brought down with it the whole side of the staircase and left a gap to the open air. Enfeebled as she still was, Beatrice managed to drag some stones out of the way and clamber over the rubble through the opening. The moat was dry, the lurid glow of the distant fires lit her on her way, and once more she set out across the wilderness: this time driven by instinct and desperation towards the one place where she knew she would find succour.

'And here I am,' she said gratefully.

'Which proves,' said Deborah, 'that you never truly believed you would be better dead. If you had, you'd not have striven so hard to live.'

★　★　★

Randall said: 'Once we heard even part of the story, we knew we must get you away from the priory.'

They sat, three of them, in a pleasant room Deborah had not seen before. She had left Beatrice sleeping soundly, and had talked away a large part of the afternoon with Randall and General Fleming. Tea had been served, Mrs. Thurton had come in to speak to Randall about something and had greeted Deborah with unexpected, spontaneous warmth; the whole atmosphere was one of calm after the storm.

Deborah felt there could yet be another storm. Justin would surely not sit back and accept defeat, especially when his intended victims were now at large, with so much to tell about him.

'I wish there were some way of laying hands on that gypsy,' said Randall thoughtfully.

The general said, 'H'm,' pessimistically. 'He'll have put a good distance between the breckland and that caravan of his. Mark you, I'd also like to get my hands on him and ask him a thing or two. I don't see how the feller could pick up a badly burnt woman off the breck at night and not find out pretty soon that there'd been a fire at Toft Warren, and put two and two together.'

'Oh, the travelling people don't gossip with the house people. And since it's clear he was poaching, he'd steer well clear of any awkward encounters. That's not why I want to talk to him. His medicines, the herbal treatments he used for those burns, and the pain reliever he administered — professional men have a lot to learn from some of these remedies.'

'Old wives' potions?' said Fleming sceptically.

'New advances in anaesthesia won't advance far enough if we turn a blind eye to what simpler and wiser folk have known for centuries.' He smiled at Deborah. 'I'm afraid you see me on my hobby horse. It has already carried me into a great deal of trouble.'

'You'll gallop out of it,' said Fleming.

Randall was still looking at Deborah. 'When I've done so . . . when I've cleared myself of the injustice that's been done to me . . . perhaps I may address myself to you. When we are both ready.'

'Damned if I see why you need wait.' The general lumbered to his feet. 'From the way you greeted this young woman when she got here, I'd say you already *had* addressed her. Good thing, too. In my day we weren't above taking on a helpmeet who'd *help*.'

With elephantine tact he plodded from the room, leaving them together.

'You mustn't take him too seriously.'

'But I do,' said Deborah. 'I never enjoyed those fairy tales of gallant knights riding off for years on some quest or other, vowing not to marry their fair maidens until they'd acquitted themselves nobly. It seemed so dull for the maidens.'

He laughed, she began to laugh with him.

Dusk crept over the grass and into the room. They talked with love, without fuss and without reservation. Candles were brought. Randall said at last that he must go to see how Beatrice was faring. As he opened the door, his bailiff was moving towards it from outside.

'Hello, Runnacre. What is it?'

'Sorry to burst in on you, sir, but I fancy there's trouble in the wind.'

'What sort of trouble?'

'A mob on its way across the breck. Coming this way, sir. I've a notion they mean us no good.'

Randall led the way out into the passage and across the hall. By the time Deborah had limped after him he had opened the door and was out on the wide top step.

A blur of shadows through the drive gates was dotted with blobs of light and a flickering of red and yellow flame. The shadows thickened into those of men walking purposefully towards the house. Some carried storm lanterns, some held reeking pitch-sodden torches aloft. On either side rode a man on horseback.

In the flare of the torches Deborah could see that the two riders were Justin Stannard and Harry Chevening.

17

The men numbered perhaps twenty. When Justin reined in his mount the whole party shuffled to a halt. In the shifting light their faces were sullen and deadly.

Randall said: 'Runnacre, give Miss Ritchie a hand up the stairs, will you?'

'I prefer to stay with you,' said Deborah.

'And I prefer that you should be with your sister. If she wakes to a deal of noise — '

'What do they intend?'

'I shall find out.'

He moved away, farther out on to the step. Reluctantly she allowed the bailiff to assist her up to Beatrice's room.

Beatrice was still asleep. Her window was ten yards or so to the left of the main entrance. Deborah could see smoke curling from the torches, and faces splotched with red and with darkness. A voice cried something and there was a muttering undertone, but she could not make out the words. Cautiously she unfastened the catch and slid the sash upwards.

Sound swelled to a menacing growl. Justin kneed his horse forward a few paces.

'To demand the surrender of those you have abducted. *That* is why we are here, and well you know it.'

Out of sight below her, Randall said: 'You're trespassing, Lord Stannard. If you wish to make a call on your own, I'm prepared to receive you. But I would ask you to send your friends off my land.'

'Drag him out,' shouted someone from the back. 'This time . . . '

Justin said: 'You're lucky I'm here, Gaunt. If you'll put yourself in Mr. Chevening's custody while I escort the ladies to safety, I'll see you come to no harm.'

'Why bring your drunken rabble in the first place?'

Deborah saw the ragged group sway, and a man stooped to pick up a stone and throw it. It thudded against the brickwork below. The mob began to tumble forward. Light fell on a waved fist and on upturned faces. In the forefront was Alfred Deeping.

Justin turned across their path and waved them back.

'I'll not condone a riot. But for your own sake, Gaunt, let yourself be removed to the town bridewell before these men take matters into their own hands.'

'On what charge?'

'Abduction! You practised evil on Beatrice Fleming, wrecked her married life and brought about the death of her husband. You drove her out on to the breck, and when she found her way into my protection you lured the poor creature away again. And my own betrothed, the woman who was pledged to marry me, as everyone well knows — what have you done with *her*?' Preaching law and order, he was calculatedly whipping up the mob at his back. 'I don't know what strange powers you have, Gaunt, but one thing I tell you tonight — you'll not dare try them on me.'

Deeping was trying to push forward. Justin was allowing himself to be edged very gradually to one side. From above Deborah could see the pattern and the turbulence that would, at a moment chosen by Justin, break loose into a wild attack on the house.

As she turned, intent on defying Randall and returning to his side, a figure brushed past her. Beatrice must have woken and slid out of bed. Before Deborah could stop her she had leaned her brow against the frame of the open window, her hands splayed out on the sill. A faint wail rose like a wisp of smoke. She had been seen.

Beatrice cried out. 'Lies, you're listening to lies. I was a prisoner, I was debauched and what he tells you is lies . . . you must *listen* . . . '

The faint, reedy cry was lost on the evening air. To those men, thought Deborah wretchedly, she must have presented a picture which fitted all Lord Stannard had said: ghostly, emaciated, fluttering vainly against a window-pane and uttering unintelligible little cries for help.

'Look at her!' Justin seized his chance. 'Now do you see? Poor demented creature, under his spell. The same spell,' he shouted, 'that he used on the woman who was to be my wife. And where is *she*? What has he done with Deborah Ritchie?'

From where she stood, Deborah could see Harry Chevening's raised head. She felt that those devilish eyes could see her, could see past Beatrice and into the room; that somehow Chevening and Justin were already hot to attack the building and race upstairs.

And then? To silence them, to say there had been a hideous accident — to blame Randall Gaunt . . . ?'

Fear and ungovernable rage had taken Justin over the borderline of sanity.

Not caring whether she was seen or not, she braced herself and tugged Beatrice forcibly away from the window.

'You must lie down. Don't you realise the harm you may have done?'

She shepherded Beatrice, dazed, back to the bed. Then she hobbled and swung herself downstairs as best she could. As she neared the foot of the stairs, the main door closed with a crash. There was a hail of stones against the woodwork. Glass shattered inwards, falling from the narrow lancet window beside the door and splintering again on the floor.

Randall stood back from the door with General Fleming beside him. The old campaigner was hunched vengefully forward as if wanting to be allowed out to hurl himself at the rabble.

The baize-covered door from the servants' quarters was pushed open. Boynton and two other men came through, each carrying shot-guns, one shouldering a musket.

'We'll not let them get into *this* house, sir.'

The general grinned round, over his shoulder. 'Reinforcements, eh?'

'Gentlemen,' said Randall. 'Have you any idea what Lord Stannard could make of this? Armed resistance to arrest . . . ? And that musket — Jellicoe, put the thing down at once. You'd blow your head off, man.'

Deborah reached him. 'You've got loyal servants,' she said.

There was a hammering at the main door.

'Gaunt! As justice of the peace for this district and with the authority of the Prosecuting Society, I order you to surrender yourself and your captives.'

Deborah said: 'Let me speak to them. I'll tell them the truth of it — make them listen.'

'You'll not go out there.'

'They couldn't hear poor Beatrice. They'll hear me.'

'You'll not be allowed to finish. Once there's a riot, you and Beatrice will be silenced — either killed in the confusion, or in some regrettable accident while he is taking you to so-called safety.'

'He must be mad to run such risks.'

'Mad,' said Randall, 'and desperate. And the greatest risk of all, so far as he's concerned, is of you and Beatrice living to tell the full tale.'

There was a renewed thumping at the door. General Fleming, without warning, stumped forward and opened it. There was a roar as he appeared, then a buzz of dissatisfaction. He was a factor they knew nothing about. Even Justin, standing on the step and apparently ready to swagger into the hall, hesitated.

Before Fleming could say whatever it was he had to say, there was a scrape of carriage wheels skidding around the gatepost and down the drive. Chevening turned his horse, incredulous. As the carriage came into the light of torches and lanterns, Deborah saw the driver's face and wondered where she had seen it before.

'Lovick, who the devil ordered you here?'

She remembered the injured child at Ingmere station. It was Chevening's coach and Chevening's coachman.

Trying to urge his horse towards the new arrival, Chevening ran it straight into the crowd. There was a resentful bellow. Their drunken mood was such that its force could swiftly be inflamed against anyone, it little mattered whom.

Isabel Stannard was descending from the carriage.

'Trouble in the enemy camp,' said General Fleming softly. 'They've lost their momentum. Fatal.'

Isabel stood below the driver's box. 'Tell them! Go on, tell them!'

'Get down, Lovick,' Chevening shouted. 'And explain yourself — to *me*.'

Lovick stood up, one hand behind him against the brass rail. 'It's *them*,' he said shakily. 'You're after the wrong man. *They're* the ones you want — Lord Stannard, and him.' His free hand waved at Chevening.

Puzzled by the general, the men were taken on the flank by Lovick. He was one of them, he spoke their own tongue. For a few undecided seconds they were bleared into attentiveness.

'Ask Lord Stannard what drove the Farren girl to do away with herself.'

'Get down, you drunken oaf.'

Lovick was gathering courage. 'Ask Mr. Chevening who helped him with weighting young Miriam down in the mere.'

Chevening kicked a man aside so that he could ride close in to his carriage. His whip slashed at Lovick's head. As the coachman ducked, Isabel tried to clutch Chevening's arm and was sent reeling.

One of the torch-bearers caught at the stallion's bridle. 'Just a minute, sir, if there's something we ought to be hearing — '

'Out of my way. If you'd take the word of a coachman with a grudge — '

'No grudge, sir.' Lovick achieved a precarious dignity as he gripped the rail and outfaced his master. 'But I'm sickened. Fair sickened.' He began to gabble at his audience before the whip should strike again. 'Many's the girl I had to fetch for them, for their dirty games in the priory. And keep quiet and ask no questions, else I was for it. The way some of those girls was for it, if they turned awkward. And there were the ones who did well for themselves, and got a fancy for it — in a mighty hurry to get off to London, that girl of yours, Fred Sulyard.'

A stooped man with a straggle of beard began to shout back, but Lovick overrode him.

'And there was worse. That child got her leg broke, that day at Ingmere. My niece, that were. An' everyone cursing Sir Randall and keeping him off like as if he was the devil. Far as Mr. Chevening was concerned, she could have died rather than have proper attention. But Sir Randall saved her, and didn't make no fuss about it.'

Deborah glanced questioningly at Randall. 'I went to see the child secretly. Sneaking to and fro like some malefactor,' he said dourly. 'But the bone will set. It was simple enough.'

Justin was moving slowly, murderously round the edge of the group towards his sister.

'And you, Isaac Farren.' The coachman's voice cracked. 'Your daughter, hanging herself like that. You know the night she was shamed into doing it? Just you think back to a Saturday night in July last year, and her telling you a fine ole taradiddle about — '

Chevening broke free and made a grab at the coachman's leg. Lovick clung to the rail for a moment, then was dragged down. He fell heavily, sprawling, to the ground. The stallion reared as if to bring its forefeet down and trample him. Justin leaped at his sister. He got one hand on her shoulder and she cried out; then a man came between her and Justin, and as he was thrust backwards, two others dragged Chevening bodily from his horse.

Deborah realised that Randall was no longer at her side. He strode down the steps, took Isabel's arm, and brought her back to the shelter of the hall.

She looked up into his face as they crossed the threshold.

'I couldn't.' She trembled. 'I couldn't let him.'

'You're safe now.'

'I knew what sort of madness would be in his mind, and . . . I couldn't let him finish it. I know you care nothing for me — ' Her gaze took in Deborah and she smiled wryly. ' — but I would not let him . . . could not . . . '

There was an ugly roar from the drive. Justin and Chevening were trying to fight their way free of the mob. Only one man stood apart, staring at Saxwold Hall, still waiting to do whatever it was he had originally come to do.

Randall snapped: 'Boynton, Runnacre — beat those fools off.'

He and three of his men hurried out, with General Fleming zestfully falling in behind them.

Isabel clung to Deborah. 'What will they . . . ?'

The lust for violence which Justin had so cunningly worked up was turned against him. These men had come here with the promise of blood, and they would not be satisfied until they had tasted it.

Randall heaved aside a man who was trying to kick Chevening, down on his knees. Boynton and Runnacre tried to batter a way through to where Justin was punching savagely and steadily at his attackers. A man went down, another tripped over him.

Suddenly there was a gap. Justin hurled himself through it. There was a howl like that of eager hounds as he raced for his horse and sprang into the saddle. Alfred Deeping, his face contorted, tried to catch Justin's leg. A boot full in his face threw him off.

Torches, thrown aside, began to crackle in the dry grass. One man, still holding

366

his burning brand, thrust it straight at Chevening. Randall snatched it away. Hoofs scrabbled on the drive, then Justin was galloping towards the gates. Men began to run after him. Chevening broke free and was running also, but managed no more than twenty yards before he was brought down again. He lay panting, his arms limp, giving up.

Justin's arm rose and fell. His horse neighed in terror, and plunged towards the gateposts. The shadows were a turmoil now. It was difficult to see which way the horse turned, or how its leg might have gone from under it. But the sound it let out was hideous, and there was a sudden baying voice from the mob and then a long, falling scream from the horse; and silence, from the animal and from the men.

Isabel pulled away from Deborah and ran out of the house, down the drive towards her brother. Deborah made the best pace she could, her stick scraping through the gravel. Two of Randall's servants were beating out a blaze started by one of the fallen torches. Smoke blew across the drive, then cleared. In a tall leap of flame, Deborah saw the hulk of the horse, twitching and trying to get up on its feet again, snorting as young Deeping approached it.

And she saw the crumpled, motionless shape of Justin Stannard. One arm was bent under him, and there was the sprawl of one leg on to the grass by the gate. His head seemed almost to lie on a pillow. But as she drew closer she saw that the pale mound was that of a large stone, darkening as a stain spread slowly from Justin's shattered head. He had come to rest on one of the eye stones laid at Randall's gates.

* * *

Dawn flooding over the breckland touched the heath with colour and etched the outlines of pine sentinels along the ridges. There had been comings and goings all night, and it was not until the whole overarching sky was aglow, and birds across the garden were in full throat, that Deborah at last found herself rubbing her eyes and yawning.

General Fleming chuckled. 'You've been determined to see it right through to the end, haven't you?'

'I don't know that I've thought of it quite like that.'

'You didn't need to think of it, gel. It's what you're made of — that's all there is to it.'

Upstairs, Beatrice slept peacefully. She had not seen the final downfall of Justin Stannard, but some inner sense must have told her that the misery was ended: her face when Deborah crept in to see her had been wiped clean of nightmare. Isabel, taken in to see her also, had at first not believed and then found it all too easy to believe. She faced up at last to truths at which she had only half guessed, not wanting or daring to guess further. Now she, too, was asleep, having been taken gently but magisterially into Mrs. Thurton's care.

Deborah sat in the study with Randall and General Fleming. They were shaken and subdued by the events of the night;

but well pleased with one another's company.

'Chevening?' she ventured. 'What will happen to him? In many ways he was the most evil thing in it. He corrupted Edwin, drove Justin on to ruin Edwin and Beatrice, enjoyed ruining Justin himself.'

'There are men now not afraid to speak out,' said Randall. 'They will be shamed into speaking out. He will face trial, and there will be no Lord Stannard to come between him and justice. The breckland wind can be a fierce one — but now I think it will be a clean one.'

'And Beatrice?'

'I think I may claim my daughter-in-law as my concern,' said Fleming gruffly. 'My son gave her no great happiness. Took a great deal from her. I think I owe it to her to look after her for a while. And then she can look after *me* for a while, till she's found her feet and I think she's fit to choose her own direction. I'll keep an eye on her, never fear.' He grinned complacently. 'Do her good. And do *me* good.'

Then the general produced an exaggerated yawn, nodded conspiratorially at Deborah, excused himself, and left them together in the obvious hope that they would continue the conversation to which he had left them the previous evening, only to be so violently interrupted.

For a while they did not speak. The room grew brighter, until the wan candle flames could be snuffed. Randall seemed to find contentment in simply looking at Deborah, and she knew that in the years to come they would be able to say so many things to each other without words.

At last he said: 'Will you hate the breckland forever?'

'Hate is something I can well do without,' she said, 'in the right company.'

'Stannard has tainted so much. The poison will linger. But this is still, in spite of everything, home for me. In time I would like it to be so for you — but only if that is what you want.'

'It will recover. A few seasons, and the poison will grow out.'

'Yes,' he said eagerly. 'Yes, I've known men to be diseased and in despair, sick with themselves and sick with life. They hate their bodies because they think their bodies have betrayed them. But when the disease has been conquered and life flows back, they learn to feel again — a wonderful time, and a dangerous time. It is so painful at first.' He looked wonderingly at her again. 'I am discovering that for myself. I need your help. I need you so much, my dearest — here, and in London, and in depths of myself I have not examined for too long.'

Deborah looked about the room and out across the sunlit awakened world. 'Wherever it may be,' she said, 'I shall be with you.'

We do hope that you have enjoyed reading this large print book.

Did you know that all of our titles are available for purchase?

We publish a wide range of high quality large print books including:
Romances, Mysteries, Classics
General Fiction
Non Fiction and Westerns

Special interest titles available in large print are:
The Little Oxford Dictionary
Music Book, Song Book
Hymn Book, Service Book

Also available from us courtesy of Oxford University Press:
Young Readers' Dictionary
(large print edition)
Young Readers' Thesaurus
(large print edition)

For further information or a free brochure, please contact us at:
Ulverscroft Large Print Books Ltd.,
The Green, Bradgate Road, Anstey,
Leicester, LE7 7FU, England.
Tel: (00 44) **0116 236 4325**
Fax: (00 44) **0116 234 0205**

Other titles in the
Linford Mystery Library:

WE MOVED IN SHADOW

Denis Hughes

Travelling north by car, David Stanmore makes a fateful stopover at a pub, where a thief steals a woman's handbag and then disappears. The distraught woman tells Stanmore that she had been on a covert mission for her employer to meet his friend in York, who was to give her information on the location of a hidden Nazi hoard of treasure. Her handbag had contained a visiting card that was to serve as her introduction. Stanmore agrees to take her in pursuit — and plunges into a nightmare world of death . . .

PERFECT PIGEON

Richard Wormser

Easy come, easy go . . . That's the life of con men who stay one step ahead of the law, two steps ahead of each other. At twenty-three, Mark Daniels embezzled his way to a cool quarter million. Sure, he got caught; that was part of his plan. All he had to do was sit tight until he could safely grab his dough. Six years later, newly released from prison, he's got his chance — but then into his lap drops the loveliest woman in the world, with the slickest murder frame he's ever seen . . .

THE VAMPIRE MAN

Gerald Verner

Conway Jackson, amateur criminologist, receives a disturbing letter from his uncle, Sir James Gleeson, informing him that he feels himself to be in terrible danger, and imploring him to come to his country manor. Unfortunately, the letter has taken some time to reach him, and it shows unmistakable signs of having been steamed open. On his arrival, Jackson learns that his uncle was found strangled in his bedroom the night before — by what appears to be an inhuman monster that is destined not to stop at a single victim . . .

MANHATTAN BOMBSHELL

Norman Firth

Reporter Larry O'Halloran has got himself a great scoop. So he's shocked when his editor refuses to run it — and no rival newspaper will touch it, either. It seems the press in this city is caught in a stranglehold, scared to print the truth, fearing retribution from a mysterious figure named 'the Raven'. So Larry starts his own paper, the *Manhattan Bombshell*, printing the stories no other sheet dares to. But the Raven will make him pay for his audacity . . .

THE LATE MRS. FIVE

Richard Wormser

Soon after Paul Porter arrives in the small rural town of Lowndesburg, he is shocked to see his beautiful ex-wife Edith getting into an expensive limousine. He discovers she is now married to rich landowner John Hilliard the Fifth, to whose mansion he makes a visit hoping to sell agricultural machinery, only to find nobody home. But the local police know of his visit — and when they discover Edith's dead body there, he becomes the prime suspect as the slayer of the late Mrs. Five!